Sandra Loved Cameron.

But a one-sided love was never, could never, be enough. Sex was one thing, love another. And Sandra knew that to hang on to one, while denying herself the other, would be self-destructive.

Her decision reached, she went in search of Cameron. And her decision was tested when she found him—all six feet four inches of gorgeous man fresh from the shower, his hair damp, his chest bare, his worn, faded jeans unsnapped....

Dear Reader,

no further! I want you to read all about what's in
re for you this month at Silhouette Desire. First, there's
the moment you've all been waiting for, the triumphant
return of Joan Hohl's BIG BAD WOLFE series! MAN
OF THE MONTH Cameron Wolfe "stars" in the absolutely
wonderful *Wolfe Wedding*. This book, Joan's twenty-fifth
Silhouette title, is a keeper. So if you plan on giving it to
someone to read I suggest you get one for yourself *and* one
for a friend—it's that good!

In addition, it's always exciting for me to present a unique
new miniseries, and SONS AND LOVERS is just such a
series. Lucas, Ridge and Reese are all brothers with a
secret past... and a romantic future. The series begins
with *Lucas: The Loner* by Cindy Gerard, and continues
in February with *Reese: The Untamed* by Susan Connell
and in March with *Ridge: The Avenger* by Leanne Banks.
Don't miss them!

If you like humor, don't miss *Peachy's Proposal*,
the next book in Carole Buck's charming, fun-filled
WEDDING BELLES series, or *My House or Yours?*
the latest from Lass Small.

If ranches are a place you'd like to visit, you must check
out Barbara McMahon's *Cowboy's Bride*. And this month
is completed with a dramatic, sensuous love story from
Metsy Hingle. The story is called *Surrender*, and I think
you'll surrender to the talents of this wonderful new writer.

Sincerely,

Lucia Macro
Senior Editor

Please address questions and book requests to:
Silhouette Reader Service
U.S.: 3010 Walden Ave., P.O. Box 1325, Buffalo, NY 14269
Canadian: P.O. Box 609, Fort Erie, Ont. L2A 5X3

Joan Hohl
WOLFE WEDDING

SILHOUETTE *Desire*®
Published by Silhouette Books
America's Publisher of Contemporary Romance

SILHOUETTE BOOKS

ISBN 0-373-05973-6

WOLFE WEDDING

Copyright © 1996 by Joan Hohl

This edition published by arrangement with Harlequin Books S.A.

® and TM are trademarks of Harlequin Books S.A., used under
license. Trademarks indicated with ® are registered in the United States
Patent and Trademark Office, the Canadian Trade Marks Office and in
other countries.

Printed in U.S.A.

Books by Joan Hohl

JOAN HOHL

has received numerous awards for her work, including the Romance Writers of America Golden Medallion award. In addition to contemporary romance, this prolific author also writes historical and time-travel romances. Joan lives in eastern Pennsylvania with her husband and family. *Wolfe Wedding* is Joan's twenty-fifth book for Silhouette.

Mrs. Maddy Wolfe

Requests the Honor of Your Company

at the Marriage of Her Son

Jake

to

Miss Sarah Cummings

on

June 12th

in the Sprucewood University Chapel at 11:00 a.m.

Luncheon Reception in Faculty Dining Room 11:30 a.m.

R.S.V.P.

One

***

Why hadn't they ever gone to bed together?

Cameron Wolfe peered over the top of his gold-framed reading glasses at the woman elegantly poised in his office doorway.

Sandra Bradley was well worth peering at.

At age thirty-one—or was it thirty-two now?—Sandra was in her glorious prime. Tall, slender, gorgeous, and smart as they came, she was one fantastic piece of work, a delight to the eyes and senses, and a worthy opponent into the bargain.

What more could any red-blooded American male ask for in a woman?

Compliance?

Cameron repressed a smile at the immediate response his brain threw out to his silent query. He could readily imagine Sandra in any role she chose to perform—any role, that is, except one of acquiescence.

An unabashed feminist and a damn sharp lawyer, Sandra was light-years beyond the outmoded traditional concept of femininity—which answered his original question about why they had never gone to bed together. He and Sandra had a professional relationship, and Cameron never mixed business with pleasure. The combination could be explosive, thus devastating. Besides, his view of women was as unabashedly traditional as Sandra's was nontraditional.

Pity.

"Well, hello," he drawled. "To what do I owe the singular honor of your visit?"

"Hello yourself." Sandra's voice always thrilled. Low and throaty, she could drawl along with the best. "It's a courtesy call." She strolled with languid grace into the room.

Attired in a severely tailored jonquil yellow suit, combined with a silk shirt, scarf, shoes and handbag in leaf green, she appeared to bring the mild freshness of Denver's early-spring weather into the room with her.

Up close, she was even easier on the eyes.

Her features were clearly classic—sculptured bone structure, beneath satiny skin with a magnolia-creamy complexion. Her well-defined, full-lipped mouth alone could have, and probably had, turned hordes of men's minds to mush, and another part of their anatomy to steel.

Her long-legged, curvaceous figure wasn't bad, either. In truth, it was muscle-clenching.

Feeling the predictable thrill, and the tightening effect, in every atom of his being, Cameron covered his reaction with the equally languid-appearing motions of first rising, then removing his glasses.

"How intriguing." He allowed a hint of a smile to shadow his lips. Laying the specs on top of the papers he had been reading, he flicked a hand to indicate the two functional chairs placed in front of his desk. "Have a seat," he said, arching one gold-kissed, tawny eyebrow. "And explain."

"The courtesy?" Matching his expression with a raised brown brow that was as dark as his were light, Sandra sank onto a chair and crossed her legs, causing her long, narrow side-split linen skirt to hitch up to reveal an enticing length of thigh.

"Er...yeah." Cameron's voice was dry, because his throat was dry, parched by the heat of his reaction to her display of one sheer-nylon-encased leg.

Lord, what his imagination could conjure around her legs, should he give it free rein. And most of the conjuring would involve those long, shapely limbs, that tapered to slender ankles, curling around him.

The fleeting thought occurred to him of how amused—surprised? shocked? amazed?—his family, friends and acquaintances would very likely be, should they be able to tap into the desire of his imagination to indulge in erotic flights of fantasy about her.

With the possible exception of his mother, who knew him best, and tended to peer beneath the surface, nearly everyone who knew Cameron believed him to be a confirmed woman-hater, as well as a confirmed bachelor.

He wasn't, of course. But having been burned once, a long time ago, he was not only wary of involvement, he was extremely selective in his choice of female companions—who had been few and far between for some years. And even then, he had never had a dalliance with anyone remotely concerned with his professional life.

Sandra, however, was something else again. There had been instances, too many for comfort, when temptation lured, desire swirled, and his imagination fought against his self-imposed control in a burning bid to soar free. To date, his control had proved stronger. Today was no different.

Imposing that hard-fought-for iron control, Cameron didn't free his imagination. With a silent sigh of regret, he reined it in instead.

"What courtesy, and why?"

Her luscious mouth curved into a knowing smile of genuine amusement, and appreciation for his discernment. Sandra had never made the mistake of taking him for anybody's fool.

"The courtesy of letting you know that you'll be getting a break from tangling with me for a while . . . possibly a long while."

He frowned; instead of clarifying, her explanation compounded his confusion. His expression mirroring his feelings, Cameron dropped into his desk chair, leaned forward and fixed a piercing stare on her.

"You want to expand on that cryptic statement?"

Sandra's smile took on a teasing quirk; her soft dark brown eyes danced with laughter lights. "You mean, what in hell am I talking about?"

Cameron gave a judicious nod of his head, and absently raised a hand to brush back the thick lock of tawny hair that tumbled onto his forehead. "Yeah, that would clear up the issue for me."

"I'm taking a leave of absence from my work and the firm," she answered with a simple candor. "A sabbatical, if you will."

Her response brought him to a full stop for an instant. The low sound of her throaty laughter jarred him out of his bemusement.

"Leave of absence?" His voice had lost the slow and easy drawl, and now held unabashed and blatant disbelief. "A sabbatical?"

Sandra made an elaborate show of glancing around the office. "Do I detect an echo in here?"

"Clever. Real clever." Cameron gave her a dry, droll look. "If you're through playing straight ma—person," he said chidingly, "are you ready to tell me what in hell you *are* talking about?"

She chided him right back. "Exactly what I said. I'm taking a leave of absence."

"Why?" His brow furrowed in a frown. "You're the best lawyer in the firm."

"Thank you for that." Sandra inclined her head in acknowledgment of the compliment. She knew they were few and far between from Cameron Wolfe.

"You're welcome. Now tell me why."

"I'm tired." Her answer came without hesitation, and with determined adamancy. "I need a break."

His eyes shadowed with brooding intent, Cameron absently toyed with one of the earpieces of his glasses as he mulled over her response.

Sandra certainly didn't look tired, he mused, studying her face in minute detail. In point of fact, she looked as bright and sparkling as the spring sunshine that was pouring through the wide office window and splashing butter yellow color on the utilitarian gray carpet.

For all the depth of his shrewd observation, Cameron could not detect the slightest sign of stress or strain in her smooth features, or in the calm, clear eyes returning his inspection.

"You don't look tired," he voiced his assessment. "Matter of fact, you look pretty good."

Sandra laughed; it was another sound that never failed to thrill. Low, throatily exciting, her laughter had always had the power to light the darkest and most secret depths of his being.

"Two compliments from you in one day." Her eyes sparkled with amusement. "Must be a record."

"A stranger overhearing you might be forgiven for thinking me some kind of ogre," Cameron said in gentle reproof. "Am I really that cold?"

"No." She shook her head, setting her sleek, stylishly bobbed sable hair swirling. "A tad remote, perhaps, but not cold." Her soft mouth curved into a teasing smile. "But for as long as I've known you, you have never been fast and loose with the compliments."

"I never saw the point in sweet-talking anyone," he said with blunt honesty.

"Yes, I know. You call them as you see them."

"Right." He gave a sharp, emphatic nod of his head, once again flipping the shock of hair onto his forehead. "So, now that we've established my forthrightness," he drawled, absently brushing back the unruly hair, "I'd like to hear the bottom-line reason for your taking a leave of absence."

Sandra shook her head despairingly, and sent another ripple of throaty laughter dancing around the room and down his spine.

"You're a hoot, Wolfe," she said, a smile remaining after her laughter subsided. "You're like a journalist in hot pursuit of a fast-breaking juicy scandal—you just don't quit, do you?"

"Quitting doesn't get you anywhere."

"Touché," she said, acknowledging his pointed barb. "But you see, the bottom line is, I am tired." A frown drew her perfectly arched brows together. "I'm more than tired. I'm burned out. I need a break."

Cameron stared at her pensively while he assimilated the depth of the shading in her voice. Sandra was saying a lot more than she was saying, he concluded, loosening his visual grip on her steadily returned stare.

"This last case get to you?" he asked, setting his reading glasses aside once more to rake long fingers through his already finger-ruffled hair.

"Yes." Her flat response was immediate, unequivocal. "It got to me."

Cameron knew the feeling; boy, did he know the feeling. The strange, almost eerie thing was, the case he had just wrapped up had gotten to him, too.

Odd, the two of them feeling the strain at the same time. Odd, and a bit weird.

He made a quick movement of his head, as if trying to shake off the uncanny sensation. Coincidence, he assured himself. Nothing but coincidence.

But was it?

Cameron's built-in computer went to work, tossing out facts and figures, irrefutable and unarguable.

He had been transferred to Denver by the Bureau the year that Sandra joined the law firm of Carlson and Carlson, a mother-and-daughter partnership handling primarily what Cameron thought of as "women's cases."

Throughout the intervening years, he had observed Sandra's dedication and work with what he hoped was a dispassionate objectivity. They had clashed and tangled on several occasions—whenever one of his cases evolved into one of her cases.

Sandra had always maintained the highest level of professionalism and the strictest moral and ethical code of behavior—as, in fact, he did himself.

In Cameron's opinion, Sandra was not just one of the best attorneys he knew but also one of the best human beings. He admired her, and genuinely liked her, more than a little—which was why he kept a professional barrier between them.

But, at the same time, he also kept close tabs on her, following her career and cases.

And her last case had been a real beaut.

Sandra had represented the mother in a child-custody battle. The divorced combatants had been equally determined to attain sole custody of the innocent party, a lovely little girl of five.

The father, one Raymond Whitfield—a man Cameron personally and secretly considered an arrogant and overbearing bastard—had been confident of winning the battle, due to his wealth and his position in the city.

The mother—made timid and fearful by years of marriage to a psychologically abusive man—had somehow worked up the courage to seek help from Carlson and Carlson, after reading an article in a national magazine about the successful record of the firm, and the skill in the courtroom of Sandra Bradley.

Sandra had not only accepted the woman as a client, she had marshaled all her formidable intelligence and talents to bring them to the case.

Sandra, the mother and, most importantly, the five-year-old child had won. The bastard had lost—with much huffing and puffing, and not a whiff of dignity.

But the battle had obviously taken a great toll on Sandra—although there was little evidence of it in her appearance or demeanor.

"He didn't lose graciously, did he?" he said, referring to the man's public harrumphing.

"No, he didn't." Sandra lifted her shoulders in a helpless shrug. "Probably because he genuinely believed he couldn't possibly lose."

"Seeing as how he comes from a very old and well-established family, with friends in high places, I suppose that's understandable."

"More like predictable," she murmured, grimacing. "He is really not a very nice man."

"Did he make any threats, open or veiled?" Cameron demanded, alerted by a hint of something in her tone, her expression.

Sandra flipped her hand in a dismissive gesture. "He was just blowing off steam."

"What did he say?"

"It wasn't important, all big—"

He cut her off, repeating his hard voiced question. "What did he say?"

"Cameron—"

He again cut her off. "Sandra. Tell me."

She heaved a sigh, but answered, "He muttered something about getting me, winning out in the end." She made a face, looking both wry and bored. "I'm sure he meant that he'd see me in court again, maybe even the Supreme Court."

"Maybe," he agreed, making a mental note to keep tabs on the man, just to be on the safe side.

"At any rate, it's over, at least for now," she said, giving him a faint smile. "And I'm tired. I've earned a break, and I'm going to take it."

"Well, at the risk of repeating myself, it doesn't show. You don't look tired."

She responded with a spine-tingling laugh.

While absorbing the effect of her laughter on his senses, Cameron couldn't help but wonder if his own weariness and uneasy sense of pointlessness were manifesting themselves in his expressions or his actions.

After more than ten years as a special agent for the Federal Bureau of Investigation, he was experiencing more than disillusionment; he was feeling jaded and cynical.

He didn't like the feeling.

Cameron sprang from a family with a history of involvement in law enforcement. Pennsylvania was his birth state. His father had been a beat cop in Philadelphia, and had been killed in the line of duty by a strung-out dealer during a narcotics bust several years ago. Cameron still ached inside at the memory.

The eldest of four sons, he was proud of his younger brothers, all three of whom were in law enforcement. The one nearest to him in age, Royce, was a sergeant with the Pennsylvania State Police.

The next brother, Eric, was on the Philadelphia police force, working undercover in the narcotics division, which he had transferred to after the death of their father. His youngest brother, Jake, after years of worrying Cameron with his rebellious attitude and footloose-and-fancy-free life-style, had finally come to terms with himself.

To the relief and delight of the entire Wolfe family, Jake had recently joined the police force in their hometown of Sprucewood, some fifteen miles from Philadelphia. In addition to settling into law enforcement, Jake had further surprised the family a short time ago by being the first one of the brothers to fall in love—really in love, seriously in love.

Baby brother Jake was getting married.

While Cameron was delighted that his brother had apparently found his niche in life and, according to their mother, whose judgment none of them ever doubted, the perfect woman to share his niche, there was a growing niggling sense of dissatisfaction inside that was beginning to concern Cameron.

Over the years, he had had some strange, even some weird, cases to contend with in his work for the Bureau. The last one in particular, which also had been wrapped up two days ago, had been both strange and weird. Disquieting, as well, since it had seemed to indicate, at least to him, the fragile mental state of the world in general, and some individuals in particular.

For weeks, while Sandra fought her case in court, Cameron had been on the trail of a real wacko, a wild and daring young man who believed himself the reincarnation of some legendary Western outlaw.

Instead of a horse, the man—who called himself Swift-Draw Slim—had jockeyed a four-wheel-drive Bronco. Slim got his kicks from holding up small-town banks throughout the Midwest and the Southwest. Which was bad enough, and reason enough to involve the FBI.

Cameron had been drawn into the case when Slim abducted a fourteen-year-old girl and took her across state lines, from New Mexico into Colorado.

Although Slim had led all the local, state and federal authorities on a merry chase, by the time he finally caught him, literally with his pants down, Cameron hadn't been laughing. In fact, he'd been mad as hell, disgusted, and about ready to throw in the towel—or throw up.

Gazing into the somber brown eyes of Sandra Bradley, Cameron suddenly decided that he needed a break, too. A sabbatical. *If you will.*

And he had accumulated vacation time due him—six weeks' time, to be exact.

He had been planning to use some of the time, two weeks or so, to fly East for his brother Jake's wedding. Jake had done him the singular honor of asking him to be his best man. The wedding was scheduled for the beginning of June, just four and a half weeks away.

But if he requested and was granted his time beginning the end of this week, which was the last full week in April, that would give him four weeks to play around with before Jake took the marriage plunge, and two weeks after the celebration to recover from the festivities.

Hmm...

His brooding gaze fixed on the delectable woman seated opposite him, Cameron mentally frowned and contemplated the advisability and possibility of playing around with Sandra Bradley.

The prospect had definite appeal, and an immediate drawback. Cameron was at once hard, hot and ready. Appearing cool, calm and in command required all the considerable control he possessed.

"I can't help wondering what you are thinking about." Amused suspicion colored Sandra's voice. "You have a decidedly devilish look about you."

Go for it.

"I was just thinking," he said, acting on the prompt that flashed through his head. "What are your plans? Anything definite in mind?"

"Yes." Sandra smiled; he swallowed a groan. "I'm going to run away, hide out for a while."

"Any particular destination?"

She nodded, setting her hair—and his insides—to rippling. "I've been given the use of a small cabin in the mountains for as long as it takes."

Cameron frowned. "For as long as it takes to do what, exactly?"

Sandra laughed. "In the words of my boss, For as long as it takes to get my head back on straight. She's convinced I simply need some breathing space."

"And it's more than that?" Cameron asked, with sudden and shrewd insight.

She hesitated, then released a deep sigh. "I honestly don't know, Cameron. I was prepared to chuck it all. I had even typed up my letter of resignation." Her lips quirked into a wry smile. "Barbara refused to accept it. In fact, she tore it in two the instant she finished reading it. That's when she handed me the keys and directions to her retreat in the mountains."

Hmm... A mountain retreat. Springtime in the Rockies. Wildflowers blooming. Birds singing. Butterflies fluttering. The alluring Sandra, and perhaps, Cameron mused, a male companion—namely him. Nature taking its course. Interesting. Exciting.

But would she?

Find out.

"Ah, when are you leaving?" he asked, in as casual a tone as he could muster.

She gave him an arch look. "The firm or the city?"

"Well . . ." Cameron shrugged. "Both."

"I've already left the firm." Her lips twitched in amusement. "On granted leave. I wanted to clean out my desk, just in case I decided to stick to my original plan not to return. Janice nearly went into a decline." She chuckled. "And Barbara wouldn't even talk about it."

"Uh-huh," he murmured, prudently keeping his opinion of the mother-daughter team to himself. After all, he cautioned himself, being brutally honest at this particular moment could hardly advance his cause.

From all indications, Sandra liked and respected both the mother and daughter of the team.

And, though he would willingly concede that they were excellent lawyers, Cameron privately considered both women, Barbara, the senior member, and her daughter, Janice, to be feminists in the extreme. Although he agreed with the concept of equality of the sexes, he did find the extremist element of the movement a bit tiring.

"Okay," he went on, "when are you planning to leave for the mountains?"

"Day after tomorrow," Sandra answered, readily enough, while fixing him with a probing stare. "Why?"

Here goes.

Cameron grabbed a quick breath.

"Want some company?"

His soft query was met by stillness. The room was still. The air was still. Sandra was the most still of all... for about ten seconds. Then she blinked, and frowned, and blurted out a choked laugh.

"You?" She stared at him in patent disbelief. "The legendary Lone Wolfe?"

"Me," he admitted. "And can the Lone Wolfe bull."

"Are you serious?" Her velvety voice had grown a little ragged around the edges.

"Quite serious," he assured her, tamping down the urge to elaborate.

"But..." She shook her head, as if trying to clear her mind, and gave another abortive laugh. "Why?"

Cameron arched a brow in chiding. "A little R and R. Fun and games. Unadulterated pleasure."

"In other words," she murmured, the ragged edges in her velvety voice smoothed out, "Sex, sex, and more sex?"

"A sensual sabbatical." Even he could hear the enticement in his soft voice. "If you will."

Two

She would!

Sandra stood beside her bed, a bemused smile curving her lips, a filmy flame red nightgown dangling from her nerveless fingertips.

Had she actually agreed to Cameron's outrageous proposal to have him stay with her in Barbara's cabin? she asked herself for perhaps the hundredth time since leaving his office a few hours ago.

In a shot!

Some folks might have accused Sandra of being aloof, but no astute person had ever accused her of being stupid—and she wasn't about to start now.

Her smile evolved into a soft, excited laugh.

It was spring. And how did the old saying go? In the spring, a young man's fancy, and all that. Well, didn't the same apply to young women, as well?

An anticipatory thrill moved through her. The filmy gown undulated through her fingers, bringing awareness of the sexy garment. Laughter again tickled the back of her throat. Contemplating the possible—hopeful?—ramifications of wearing the revealing scrap of nothing for him, she folded the nightie and tucked it into the suitcase lying open on her bed.

Imagine, she mused, the legendary Lone Wolfe expressing a desire to spend time in seclusion for an unspecified time...with her!

Wild.

How long had she been secretly lusting for the oh-so-cool-and-self-contained Cameron Wolfe?

Sandra laughed once more, low and sultry. She knew full well how long it had been. She had wanted Cameron from the very first day she met him, six long years ago. And wanting him had ruined her chances of forming a deep romantic relationship with any other man.

From the very beginning, it had had to be Cameron, or no one. And the passage of time had not diminished her desire for him. On the contrary, getting to know him, learning about some of the facets of his character—his honesty, his high personal moral code, his dedication to duty—had only deepened the attraction she felt for him.

She wanted him, and it was as simple as that. Foolish, maybe, but that was the way it was.

And now...and now...

Anticipation expanded into an effervescent sensation inside her, rushing through her bloodstream, intoxicating her mind and senses. Reacting to the stimulant, she turned and two-stepped across the room to her dresser, pulling open the drawer containing her mostly ultrafeminine lingerie.

Humming an old and very suggestive love ballad, she moved around the room, from the dresser to the closet to the bed, with side trips into the bathroom, filling the suitcase and a large nylon carryon with the things she wanted to take to the cabin.

Originally thinking to do nothing more strenuous than take short, brisk hikes in the foothills surrounding the cabin, Sandra had planned on packing only what she thought of as loafing-around clothes—jeans, sweatshirts, sweaters, parka, boots and such. But at one point, while she was removing an old cotton shirt, soft from many washings, from the closet, her glance had touched, then settled on, a new, more alluring outfit.

Sandra had never worn the two-piece ensemble. It bore a Paris label—a thirty-second-birthday gift she had received over a month ago from her parents, who were spending a year in France, both working and having a grand time, while her father set up international offices there for his business firm.

The reason Sandra had never worn the outfit was that there had never been an occasion suitable for her to do so. The set was too darn alluring for just any old gathering of friends.

Fashioned of sand-washed silk in shimmering swirls of fuchsia, orange and mint green, the outfit consisted of a voluminous-sleeved poet-style shirt and a belted, full-flowing skirt.

Viewed on a padded clothes hanger, the ensemble appeared innocent enough. But, upon trying it on for fit, Sandra had been mildly shocked by the appearance she presented in it.

The first button on the shirt was placed at mid-chest, a plunging vee revealing the cleavage of her high, fully rounded breasts. And, although there was an abundance of material to the skirt, when she moved, it swirled around her long legs, the clinging silk caressing every curve from her waist to her ankles.

At the time, Sandra had stared at her mirrored image in wide-eyed amazement, deciding on the spot that the outfit was too blatantly sexy for just any casual get-together. It was definitely for something special.

An impish glow sparkled in her dark eyes now as a thought flashed through her mind.

The Lone Wolfe was someone special. And being with him would most definitely be special.

Sandra carefully folded the two pieces and tucked them into the case.

How much farther could it possibly be?

Sandra frowned as she maneuvered her one-year-old front-wheel-drive compact around yet another sharp bend in the narrow, rutted, mud-and-slush-covered dirt road. Although spring had arrived at the lower elevations, shallow mounds of snow still lay in patches on the ground and beneath the trees in the foothills of the mountain range northwest of Denver.

A quick glance at the dashboard clock told her that thirty-odd minutes had elapsed since she had made the turn off the major highway indicated in the directions Barbara had written down for her.

By Sandra's reckoning, she should soon be seeing the signpost indicating the private road leading to the cabin. Even though she knew what to expect, she laughed aloud upon sighting the sign with the words *Escape Hatch* printed in bold letters on it.

The private driveway leading to the cabin was in worse condition than the dirt road, the slush concealing potholes that caught her unawares and caused the vehicle to lurch from side to side.

Sandra heaved a deep sigh of relief when the cabin came into view around a gentle curve in the road.

Seemingly built into the side of the hill, the log cabin looked as if it belonged there, nestled in amid the tall pines. A broad porch fronted the cabin. A wide window overlooked the porch and the valley beyond.

Anxious to see the inside of the place, Sandra stepped from the vehicle and tramped through the diminishing snow cover to the three broad steps leading up to the porch. The sunshine was warm on her shoulders, and turned the snow to mush beneath her hiking boots.

Around the base of the cabin, yellow and white jonquils raised their bright faces to the spring sunlight, while at the base of the stalks, shoots of delicate green grasses poked through the melting snow.

Smiling at the harbingers of spring, Sandra mounted the stairs to the porch and strode to the front door, key at the ready. Unlocking the door, she turned the knob, pushed open the door, stepped inside, and came to an abrupt halt, a soft "Oh..." whispering through her parted lips.

The cabin was everything she had dared to hope for, and more. Barbara had warned that the place was rustic, and it was. And yet the decorative touches—a flower-bedecked, deep-cushioned sofa and two matching chairs, sun yellow curtains, and a large rug braided in colors harmonizing with those in the furniture and the curtains—gave the place a snug, homey warmth, even though the still air inside felt at least ten degrees colder than the spring-washed air outside.

Sandra longed to investigate, but, deciding to deal with first things first, went directly to the thermostat to activate the heater, which, Barbara had assured her, had a full supply of fuel. Hearing the heater kick on, she turned and retraced her steps outside to collect her gear and the groceries she had purchased before leaving the city.

In all, four trips were required from the cabin to the vehicle, and Sandra was panting for breath by the time she set the last two bags of groceries on the butcher-block table in the small kitchen.

Whew! Was she getting old—or was she just terribly out of shape?

Pausing to catch her breath, she ran a slow, comprehensive look over the room. Her perusal banished consideration of encroaching age and deteriorating physical condition. A smile of satisfaction tilted her lips at what she observed.

Though small, the kitchen was compact, every inch of space wisely utilized, with fitted cabinets above and below the sink, and a small electric range and refrigerator. A full-size microwave oven was tucked into a corner of the countertop, and next to it sat the latest in automatic coffeemakers. A small, uncurtained window above the sink looked out over a smaller replica of the front porch, and the stately pines dotting the gentle incline of the foothills. A bottled-gas-fired grill stood on the wood-railed porch. Its domed lid wore a thin layer of snow.

Hmm... Sandra's mouth watered as she envisioned the steaks she'd bought, sizzling to a perfect medium-rare on the grill. Thinking of the steaks brought awareness of place and time—and it was time to put the food away, unpack her cases and familiarize herself with the place that would be her home for several weeks.

But first, she could do with a cup of coffee.

Humming softly, she washed the glass pot, then dug out of a stuffed-full grocery bag one of the cans of French-roast coffee she had bought. While the aromatic stream of dark liquid trickled into the pot, she loaded perishable foods—meat, cheese, eggs, milk, and fresh vegetables and fruits—into the fridge. Onto the bottom shelf she slid the two bottles of wine, one white, one red, that she had thought to pick up. The dried and canned articles went into the overhead cabinets.

When the foodstuffs were stashed away, Sandra poured coffee into a rainbow-decorated ceramic mug and carried it into the cabin's single bedroom, where she had earlier dumped her suitcase and carryon, and the shopping bag into which she had jammed sheets and towels.

Measuring approximately twelve feet by fourteen, the room was far from spacious. And yet the sparse furnishings, a double bed, a small nightstand and one standard-size chest of drawers, lent the illusion of roominess.

Another brightly colored braided rug covered most of the pine board floor. As in the living room, the colors in the rug were picked up in the bedspread and curtains at the room's two windows, one of which faced the north side of the cabin, the other the mountains to the rear.

All in all, not bad, Sandra decided, hefting the large suitcase onto the bed, then plopping onto the mattress and bouncing to test the resiliency of the springs.

It would do quite adequately, she thought, shivering in response to the thrill of anticipation that scurried up her back as an image of Cameron Wolfe filled her mind, along with the realization of what the bed would be used for, besides sleeping.

The temptation was overwhelming to forget every other concern and to settle back, wallowing in the comfort of the mattress... and exciting speculation.

But, being disciplined and responsible, Sandra resisted the temptation. With an unconscious sigh of longing, she heaved herself from the bed.

It was now midafternoon on Thursday, and there was work to be done before Cameron's scheduled arrival. He had told her to expect him sometime around noon, give or take an hour or so, on Saturday.

Sandra flicked the clasps on the large suitcase and flipped it open. She had to get her tush in gear. She had to unpack, put away her clothes, make up the bed with her own sheets. And then start scrubbing.

Barbara had given Sandra fair warning that, as she hadn't been to the cabin since the beginning of December, the place would need a thorough cleaning.

Barbara had not been overstating the case. Even with her quick initial perusal of the place, Sandra had noted the layer of dust that coated every flat surface, lamp, appliance and knickknack...not to mention the tile and fixtures in the bathroom.

It was immediately obvious that neither Barbara nor her daughter was very neat or very much inclined toward cleaning up after themselves. Fortunately, that was not reflected in their professional work or their workplace.

But at the time of her employer's offer, delighted with the idea of having the use of the isolated retreat, Sandra had shrugged and readily agreed to doing the necessary work involved.

Still, being willing to do the housekeeping chores and actually doing the work were two entirely different things, especially when one was not, either by nature or by training, particularly domesticated.

Sandra heaved another sigh as she began removing her clothes from the case. She did not *do* housework. With the jam-packed client schedule she carried—or had been carrying up until now—she didn't have time to do housework, even if she was so inclined. She paid a hefty amount to a professional service to *do* for her.

But the cleaning service was in Denver, and she was here, in this isolated cabin. So, Ms. Professional, she told herself, systematically stowing her things in dresser drawers and closets, you'd be well advised to get your act together and get it done.

Sandra was nearly undone herself when she pulled open the narrow drawer in the bedside nightstand. As small as it was, the gun inside the drawer looked lethal—which, of course, it was.

Naturally, she had known it was there. Barbara had told her it was there. Still...

Sandra hated guns. She knew how to handle them, how to use them properly, simply because the use of them had been included in a self-defense class she took while in college. Even so, she hated them.

Shuddering, she slipped the paperback novels she'd brought with her into the drawer, shoving the weapon, and the accompanying box of cartridges, to the back, out of sight. Then, firmly erasing the ugly thing from her thoughts, she turned to begin working on the bed.

Did she want Cameron to think she was a slob?

"Your man flew out of Denver in a private plane at 6:35 this morning."

"Heading where?" Cameron asked tersely into the phone. He slanted a glance at his watch. It read 6:51; his operative was right on top of his assignment, as he had fully expected him to be.

"Chicago."

Cameron breathed a sigh of relief; if Whitfield was off to Chicago, on business or whatever, he couldn't very well be harassing Sandra.

"Thanks, Steve," he said. "Who will take over surveillance there?"

"Jibs."

"Okay. I'll be out of town for a couple of weeks, but I'll be in touch."

"I'll be here." Steve hesitated, then asked, "You going on assignment or vacation?"

"Vacation."

Steve let out an exaggerated groan. "I should be so lucky. Enjoy."

A slow smile played over Cameron's lips as an image of Sandra filled his mind.

"Oh, I intend to," he said, anticipation simmering within him. "Every minute."

After cradling the receiver, he shot another look at his watch. It read 6:59. He had another call to make, back East, but it was still too early.

Turning away from the kitchen wall phone, Cameron poured himself a fresh cup of coffee, then headed for the bedroom. He also still had some packing to finish, the last-minute things he had left for this morning. Sipping the hot brew, he sauntered into his bedroom.

Pack first, call later.

The job of finishing up the packing required all of thirteen and a half minutes—Cameron was nothing if not both neat and efficient.

In addition to being a supremely competent and confident law-enforcement agent, recognized as one of the best operatives in the field, he was a proficient cook *and* did his own laundry.

Cameron was firmly convinced that his talents when it came to law enforcement were in his genes—although he was the first to credit his father for his early training along those lines.

But his domestic talents were definitely attributable to the concentrated efforts of his indomitable mother. From day one, son one, Maddy Wolfe had stoutly maintained that any idiot could learn to pick up after himself, and that included each one of her sons.

Having lived a bachelor existence from the day he left home for college, at age eighteen, Cameron had numerous times given fervent, if silent, thanks to his mother for her persistence.

He had spent more than a few day-off mornings on his knees, scrubbing the kitchen or bathroom floor of whatever apartment he happened to be living in at the time.

Though this was one of his days off, both his kitchen and bathroom floors were spotlessly clean, as was everything in his current apartment, thanks to the professional housekeeper he now paid to do the chore.

He shot yet another quick look at his watch; all of five minutes had elapsed since his last look. What to do? He had made his bed over an hour ago and, except for washing up the few dishes he had used for breakfast, there was really nothing left to do.

So, wash the dishes.

Draining the swallow of coffee remaining in the cup, Cameron left the bedroom and headed for the kitchen. Fifteen minutes later, with the dishes done and put away, and finding himself wiping the countertop for the third time, he literally threw in the sponge, or in this case the abused dishcloth.

Impatience crawled through him. He fairly itched to go, from the apartment, out of the city, into the foothills, in a beeline to Sandra.

Although he had committed them to memory, he dug from his pocket the piece of paper on which he had jotted Sandra's directions to the cabin. A piece of cake, he decided, tossing the scrap of paper on the sparkling clean table.

Now what? Cameron heaved a sigh and sliced a glaring glance from the clock to the phone.

The hell with it. Early or not, he was placing the call.

Maddy answered on the second ring. "Hello?"

"Good morning, beautiful," Cameron said smoothly, heaving another silent sigh of relief at the wide-awake sound of his mother's voice. "How are you on this bright spring morning?"

"It's storming here, but I'm fine, just the same," she returned dryly. "How are you?"

"As usual," he answered—as usual. "I didn't wake you, did I?"

"Wake me?" Maddy laughed; it was a rich, deep sound that he had always loved. "I've been up for hours. But you did catch me in the middle of mixing pie crust."

"Pie crust." Cameron mentally licked his lips; Maddy did make tasty pies. "For shoofly?" Shoofly pie was his all-time favorite.

She laughed again—a mother's laugh. "No. Not today. I'm making lemon meringue." She chuckled again, and this time the sound was different, loaded with amusement and self-satisfaction.

Cameron frowned. What was she up to? He knew full well that lemon meringue was his brother Eric's all-time favorite. But why should that amuse his mother?

"Eric coming for dinner?"

"Not today. Tomorrow," she said, and now her voice was rife with an alerting . . . something.

"Okay, Mom, I give up," he said, his curiosity thoroughly aroused, as he knew she had deliberately set out to do. "What's the story with Eric?"

"He's coming for dinner tomorrow."

Maddy did so enjoy teasing her overgrown sons—teasing and testing.

Despite his impatience to get under way, Cameron had to laugh, enjoying his mother's enjoyment.

"And?" he prompted when she failed to continue.

"He's bringing Tina with him."

Tina. He should have known. Cameron administered a mental self-reprimand for missing the clue Maddy had given him.

Lemon meringue. Not only was the dessert Eric's favorite, but also, from what Maddy had told Cameron, the object of a friendly rivalry between his mother and the young woman his brother had met last fall.

At Maddy's invitation, Eric had brought the woman home to meet her at Thanksgiving. Tina had brought along a lemon meringue pie as her contribution to the feast.

After the holiday, when Maddy relayed the information to Cameron, she had graciously conceded that Tina's pie was first-rate...almost as good as her own.

Cameron hadn't been fooled for a moment. He knew at once that Maddy didn't give a rip about the pies, one way or the other. But what she did care about was the possibility of a serious relationship growing between Eric and Tina, who, she claimed, was a lovely young woman.

Cameron was also fully aware that his mother lived in hope of first seeing her sons settled into marriages as strong as her own had been, and second spoiling the hell out of her grandchildren—of whom she had expressed a desire for at least eight.

And now Eric was bringing the woman home to mother for a second visit.

Hmm, he mused, recalling that, to his knowledge, Eric had never brought a woman home twice.

First Jake. Now Eric?

"Does this portend something?" he asked after a lengthy silence, realizing that his mother had calmly been waiting for him to assimilate the facts.

"I sincerely hope so," she answered. "Keep in touch, and I'll keep you informed."

"Yeah, well, as to that," he said, interested in being brought up to speed on his brother's love life, but a lot more interested in pursuing his own, "I'm not sure when I'll be able to get back to you. I'm going out of town for a spell."

"I see." Not a hint of concern tainted her voice; after thirty years of living with a police officer, she had long since learned to conceal her fears. "Well, then, I'll talk to you when I talk to you." She paused, then added softly, "Take care, son."

"I will." A gentle smile tugged at his lips as he hung up the phone. In his admittedly biased opinion, Maddy epitomized the best of the female sex.

Female.

Sex.

Sandra.

Swinging away from the phone, Cameron strode from the kitchen. He collected his bags, glanced at, then deliberately shifted his gaze away from his beeper, which was lying atop the bedside table. He wouldn't need that where he was going. Gear in hand, he gave a final sweeping look around the room, then left the apartment.

"Dammit." Cameron wasn't even aware of swearing aloud; he was too busy making the turn to head back. He had driven only a few miles from his apartment when he knew he just couldn't do it. He just could not leave town for two weeks without his "connection" to the office, and the weapon that had grown to feel almost a part of him.

Muttering to himself that the two items had taken on the semblance of adult pacifiers, he strode into the apartment and directly to the bedside table.

After snatching up the beeper and the shoulder-holstered agency-issue revolver, he shoved the beeper into his pocket and, gripping the weapon, pivoted and retraced his steps to the door.

Something, an uneasy sensation, halted him midway to the door. What was it? he asked himself, raking the living room with a narrowed look. What was wrong? Nothing had been disturbed in the bedroom. Pacing to the kitchen, he ran a slow, encompassing look around. The entire place was exactly as he'd left it a half hour ago.

Still...

Sandra.

Telling himself he really did need a vacation, Cameron shrugged off the odd sensation, patted his pocket and once again exited the apartment. After stashing the gun in the rear of the vehicle, he drove away.

Now he was on vacation.

Maybe he'd stop somewhere along the way to the cabin and pick up a bottle or two of good wine, and a couple of six-packs of beer, he mused, anticipation crawling along his nerve endings, arousing all kinds of wicked thoughts and exciting reactions.

It wasn't until he was well out of the city, the wine and beer stashed in the back of his almost new Jeep Cherokee, that Cameron gave some thought to his brothers—and one in particular.

While talking to his mother, he had mused about his brothers. First Jake, the baby of the Wolfe pack, and now Eric, the third of the brood. But, on reflection, he recollected a phone conversation that he had had several weeks ago with Royce.

At the time, something—more what Royce hadn't said than what he had, a trace of distraction in his manner—had bothered Cameron.

Now, on reflection, he wondered whether Royce could possibly be involved with a woman, and whether his emotions were seriously engaged. Of course, he could have been reading his brother's voice incorrectly. But Cameron seriously doubted it; he knew his brothers.

And now, here he was, impatiently maintaining the legal speed limit, as anxious and excited as a teenager in the first throes of passion about spending a couple weeks alone in the mountains with Sandra.

Hmm...

Did this portend something?

Cameron's question to his mother came back to haunt and taunt him.

It's physical, my attraction to Sandra is purely physical, he assured himself, while trying to ignore the tingle that did a tango from his nape to the base of his spine.

Wasn't it?

Three

"Whoosh..." Sandra exhaled a deep breath and swiped the back of her hand across her damp forehead.

Damn, housecleaning was hard work, she thought, but at last she was finished. The interior of the cabin virtually sparkled as a result of her concentrated efforts of yesterday afternoon and all of today.

Going into the now-gleaming kitchen, she crossed to the fridge for a diet cola. She was sweaty. She was thirsty. She was hungry. And, boy, was she tired.

Was Cameron Wolfe worth her feverish flurry of activity? Sandra asked herself, dropping limply onto a lemon-scented, polished chair.

Damned right he was!

Laughing to and at herself, she downed the last of the cola and heaved her wilting body from the chair.

Tomorrow.

Cameron should—would—be arriving in less than twenty-four hours.

An anticipatory chill invaded her body.

It was rather shocking. Sandra scowled at herself, at her involuntary physical and emotional response to the mere thought of Cameron's forthcoming arrival.

Honestly, she chided herself. If her thoughts, feelings, could have been monitored, a stranger, or friend, could have been forgiven for looking askance at her. She was a full-grown woman, mature, intelligent—well, usually. And here she stood, shivering, in the center of the kitchen, figuratively and literally itching to get her hands, among other body parts, on Cameron Wolfe.

Pitiful.

Sandra grinned.

So it was pitiful. So what?

She wanted the Lone Wolfe in the worst way... and the best way... every way there was.

Hell, for all she knew, maybe she was actually in love with the man.

Now there was a sobering speculation. Sobering and scary. Who knew what love was? Or even if love, romantic love, really existed outside the fantasies individuals dreamed up for themselves?

Sandra had never run across that impossible-to-describe, elusive emotion.

The affliction called love certainly couldn't be clinically diagnosed. Nor could it be smeared on a slide and studied under a microscope. Come to that, as far as Sandra knew, the feverish fancy had never been nailed down by an absolute definition.

That being the case, how was one woman supposed to know if and when the emotion struck, replacing common sense with uncommon appetites?

Appetites.

Her stomach rumbled.

There were appetites, and then there were appetites.

Sandra laughed aloud. Here she stood, quite like a twittery teenager, mooning over a man, when what she should be doing was rustling up some food.

Of course, Sandra was well aware that feeding herself, getting a shower, shampooing her sweat-stiffened hair, then having a good night's sleep, were all ploys to distract herself from contemplation.

She didn't want to think about love, in any way, shape or form.

Sex, yes.

But love?

That really was too scary.

Sandra did sleep well, surprisingly well, considering her mental upheaval during the hours prior to her crawling between the sheets.

The questions of the evening, most especially the questions about motivation, were banished by the exciting, erotic dreams that visited her in slumber.

She awoke refreshed, eager to embrace the bright spring morning, and the man who hopefully would be joining her in the retreat by lunchtime.

After a leisurely breakfast of juice, toast and coffee, Sandra switched on the radio, and proceeded to while away the hours by alternately pacing from room to room and staring out the wide front window and along the road leading to the cabin.

He was late.

It was past noon.

Had he changed his mind?

Sandra bit her lip and peered down the driveway.

It was exactly 12:46 when she spied his Jeep; Sandra knew, because she shot a quick look at her wristwatch as she made a dash for the door to greet him.

She stepped onto the deck as Cameron stepped from the Jeep. The sun felt warm on her face. The sight of him made her feel warmer all over.

The Lone Wolfe.

Lord! He looked delicious.

Good enough to eat.

Sandra promised herself a taste.

He was dressed for the outdoors—tight jeans, denim jacket and desert boots. He waved and strode toward her, looking long and lean and dangerous.

Sandra shivered in the sunshine.

"Hi."

Cameron's voice, low, intimate, was more dangerous than the look of him. Her pulse leaped. Her heartbeat went thumpety-thump. Her breath fluttered from between her parted lips on a whisper.

"Hi."

He took the steps in two long bounds.

Nervous as a crab dodging a rake, she skittered sideways to the door. "Come in."

He was right behind her.

The strains of an old love ballad blared from the radio. She started toward it to turn down the volume. One step, and then: "Oh!" She yelped as a strong arm curled around her waist, turning her around, bringing her hard against his harder body.

"Dance with me, I want my arms about you...."
He sang along with the instrumental rendition of
the song in a low, seductive voice.

Sandra gave herself up to the moment, and the
dance, and the thrill of moving in time with him.

They danced together very well, as if they had
been doing it for years. Bemused, beguiled, Sandra found herself thrilling to the prospect of their
being so attuned to one another in the more intimate dance of love.

"I'm hungry," the Lone Wolfe growled into her
ear.

She shivered. "I . . . I'll make you lunch."

"I don't think so." His soft laughter was pure
incitement. "I'll have you for lunch."

"M-m-m-me?" Sandra drew her head back to
stare at him; the raw passion blazing from his eyes
ignited a liquid fire in the core of her, and burned
her inhibitions to smoldering flinders.

"You. Me." He trailed a hand down to the hol-
low at the base of her spine, aligning her body to
the fullness of his. "Let's feast on each other." His
warm breath caressed her lips as he slowly lowered
his head.

Barely breathing, Sandra parted her lips an instant before his mouth touched hers. His lips were
firm, still cool from the outdoors and sweet with
the taste of spring.

She moaned and raised her arms to capture his head in her hands.

His tongue dipped, then dipped lower still to her throat.

Her fingers dug into the thick strands of his hair, tugging him closer, closer.

His free hand teased the outer curve and the underside of her breast.

She arched her back, inviting exploration.

His lips hardened, plundering her soft mouth as his hand curled around the soft mound.

She shuddered at the sensations caused by his teasing fingers, and scraped her nails against his scalp, from crown to nape.

"Yes."

She felt his response, whispered into her mouth, leaping against her body.

"Yes," she replied in kind, murmuring into his mouth, arching into his arousal.

In a haze of desire, time lost relevance. Their clothing was swept away, unnoticed, unmissed.

"The bed?" Cameron's lips moved around the tightness of one nipple.

"This way." Grasping his hand, she stepped back, and turned toward the hallway.

Scooping up his jeans from the floor, Cameron followed her to the bedroom.

Neither noticed nor cared that the front door was left standing wide open.

She released his hand by the side of the bed, then stepped back to look at him.

Unembarrassed in his nakedness, the Lone Wolfe stood tall and proud, magnificent in his masculine glory.

He was beautiful. Sandra's throat and lips suddenly felt hot and dry. She skimmed her tongue over her lips to moisten them.

"You're beautiful." His voice was rough-edged, exciting in its intensity.

"So are you." Her voice was barely audible.

He smiled.

She raised a hand to stroke his chest; her fingers tingled to touch the tight whorls of dark burnished-gold hair. Emboldened by the tremor her touch sent through him, she slowly skimmed her fingers down the narrowing trail of hair, to flatten her palm against the tightening muscles of his concave belly.

Cameron sucked in his breath. "Don't stop there," he said in a raw whisper. "Please, don't stop there. Find me. Hold me."

Watching the fire of desire leap higher in his eyes, Sandra glided her hand lower, through the silky curls surrounding his manhood. He moaned and shuddered when her fingers encased him.

"Good. That feels so unbelievably good." Cautioning, "Don't let go," he moved closer to her and, cradling her breasts in his hands, bent his head to suckle each rigid nipple in turn.

Responding to the sensations rioting inside her, the heat building in the core of her femininity, Sandra arched into his hungry mouth and caressed his silky-smooth, throbbing flesh.

Her mind, her body, every atom and molecule of her, was ready for him when he coiled an arm around her waist and lowered her to the edge of the bed. Before she realized what he was doing, he'd dropped to his knees between her parted, quivering thighs.

"Cameron?" She protested when he grasped her shoulders and gently moved her back, onto the mattress. "What are you doing?" she said raggedly when he pressed his lips to her belly, stabbed his tongue into her navel.

"I want to taste you," he murmured against her skin, moistening it as he slid his tongue lower. "Every sweet, intoxicating inch of you."

"Cameron." Though her voice betrayed the uncertainty she was feeling, her hands speared into his hair, anchoring his head to her body.

"You'll love it," he promised, swirling his tongue around the tight curls covering her mound. "I'm going to send you soaring."

Sandra could hear her own harsh breaths, and knew they were caused by anticipation, not trepidation. She had never allowed this intimacy, never granted the right to any other man.

But this was Cameron. The Lone Wolfe. A man of the law, and a law unto himself.

His tongue tasted the moist heat of her.

Sandra surrendered herself to the law.

Moments later, Cameron delivered on his promise. Ripples of unimagined and unimaginable pleasure cascading through her, Sandra went soaring into the no-time, no-space realm of ecstasy.

The flight was spectacular, but it soon became apparent to Sandra that the journey into sensuality was far from over.

Cameron had an agenda of his own to pursue.

Vaguely, at the fringes of her consciousness, Sandra heard the faint rustle of clothing, the quick, distinctive sound of foil being ripped. Then he was looming over her, moving her limp, depleted body lengthwise onto the bed, settling his taut-muscled form between her thighs.

"That was beautiful to watch," he murmured, stroking the tremor from her legs. "You're beautiful to watch." He slid his hands beneath her and raised her hips, aligning her body with the probing tip of his manhood. "Now, I want to watch you do it again, with me."

Sandra knew it was possible; at least she had heard it was possible, although she had never experienced the sensation of a repeat release. In truth, she had only ever experienced a single release, on a rare occasion. But, grateful for the exquisite pleasure he had given to her, she was willing to try, to be the vessel of his ultimate release and pleasure.

He entered her slowly, delicately, allowing her still-pulsating body to adjust to the fullness of his, making her feel treasured, not at all a mere vessel, a convenient depository for his passion.

To Sandra's surprise, her own desire flared anew when he began to move, carefully pacing his rhythm to her response, tightly reining his own needs, while fanning the flames of the smoldering spark of passion.

The look of him enhanced the tension spiraling inside her. In the throes of rigidly controlled passion, Cameron was a sight to behold.

His hair was ruffled from his earlier attention to her pleasure, one gold-streaked swath sweeping his forehead. His eyes were narrowed, intent on the emotional reactions revealed in her expression. His face was strained, and his bared teeth were clenched in determination. The strain was reflected in the tendons and veins throbbing in his arched throat, the muscles bunched in his chest.

He was working, hard, denying himself the soaring experience in an effort to stir her to the point of flying with him.

Beads of sweat stood out on his forehead and darkened his hair. His sun-bronzed skin shimmered, slick and moist from perspiration. His flat belly slid, wet and silky, against hers.

Everything about him, the look of him, the intensity he revealed, heightened the tension, the excitement revitalizing her, driving her to match his ardor.

She could barely breathe, and yet she felt exhilarated. The muscles in her body, which had felt slack and weak moments ago, now felt strong, energized.

Tightening her legs around his thighs, Sandra grasped his hips and arched high, into the measured rhythm of his thrusting body.

Without missing a beat of his driving motion, Cameron suddenly lowered his head to her breast, to capture one turgid nipple between his teeth.

The sensations his nipping teeth created inside her tore a gasping moan from her throat. Her heartbeat thrummed against her eardrums. Her pulses stampeded. Her body clenched around him.

A low, growl-like sound rumbled deep in his throat. "If you do that again, I can't be held accountable," he warned, in a harsh, tension-strained whisper.

A sense of sheer feminine power filled Sandra. Testing him, his control, she sank her nails into the spare flesh stretched over his hipbones, and this time deliberately clenched around him.

"Sandra, have mercy," he pleaded, teeth snapping together, veins now prominent in his forehead.

Once again she clenched, inwardly drawing on him. In response, Cameron thrust to the hilt, while simultaneously thrusting a hand between their bodies to stroke the aroused center of her femininity.

"Wolfe!" Crying his name in a strangled exclamation, Sandra went off like a rocket, blasting into space, convulsing wildly around him.

Within a heartbeat, she heard her own name cried in a harsh exaltation of joy, and felt the throbbing heat of his powerful release.

Sandra was exhausted. Every muscle and nerve in her body quivered. She could hardly breathe. She felt drained, hot and wet. Cameron's weight crushed her, pressing her into the damp sheet beneath her.

It was wonderful.

"Now...that's...what I call...a greeting," he said, between harsh gasps for breath. His tongue swept over her nipple, sending a shiver cascading through her. "And one spectacular way to begin a vacation."

Startled by the instant response of her body to the caress of his lips, Sandra gasped and wriggled her hips; his response was just as instantaneous. She felt the leap of life deep within her.

"Again?" Awe colored her tone, and surprise widened her eyes as she met the glittering gaze he fixed on her.

"Amazing, ain't it?" Laughter, and more than a hint of masculine pride, threaded his voice. "Are you game for another gallop?"

"That depends on the inducements offered to me to ride," she rejoined, laughing along with him.

"Suppose I say please?" he asked, but without giving her time to answer, he heaved himself up and over, hauling her with him.

Sandra found herself in the saddle—so to speak. "Please would be nice," she said, drawing a moan from him by settling onto his hair-roughened thighs, and settling him firmly inside her.

"Please, Sandra," he said, retaliating by arching high off the bed, thrusting deeply into her. "Ride with me into the fires of ecstasy."

Before many more moments elapsed, it was Sandra who was crying "Please" and "More" and "Hurry" and then "Oh, Cameron, Cameron!"

Four

Sandra surfaced from a light doze to the tingling sensation of long fingers combing through her hair.

She curled closer to the man beside her, to press her lips to his chest.

The combing fingers stilled. The chest beneath her parted lips expanded.

"I'm sorry if I woke you." Cameron's warm breath ruffled her hair, and her pulse.

"S'okay," she mumbled, in a voice still slurred by sleep. She yawned, and felt a tremor ripple through him from the movement of her mouth against his skin. "It's chilly in here." Sandra shivered, then frowned. "Where is that cool air coming from?"

"I'm afraid we left the front door wide open," he said, moving away from her to first pull the comforter over her trembling body, then roll off the bed. "I guess I'd better go shut it before we find ourselves sharing the place with little forest critters."

The possibility held very little appeal for Sandra. "Critters?" she yelped, tossing back the comforter and springing to her feet. "What kind of critters?" she cried, scurrying about to find her robe.

"Oh, squirrels, and raccoons, and skunks, and . . . maybe a snake or two."

Turned away from him, she didn't see the devilish gleam in his eyes, but she couldn't miss the laughter threaded through his voice. Even so, she responded to his teasing bait.

"Snakes!" She whipped around to stare at him in abject horror. "Do you really think—?"

"No, of course not," Cameron quickly interrupted to reassure her. "I was only teasing."

"Teasing? You, you—" She burst out laughing, while trying to sound angry. Unsuccessful at her attempt to appear incensed, she threw her robe at him.

Laughing with her, and nimbly stepping out of the line of fire, Cameron made a hasty retreat from the room.

He should have looked ludicrous, trotting through the doorway as naked as a newborn, Sandra mused, staring after him. But he didn't. Quite the contrary, she realized. To her eyes, he appeared utterly natural, in his element, breathtaking and magnificent.

The Lone Wolfe.

Sandra shivered; her reaction owed nothing to the chill in the spring air.

"Is it safe for me to come in?" Cameron called from the hallway. "Or are you clothing-armed and to be assumed dangerous?"

"I'm unarmed, Officer," she called back, suppressing an urge to giggle like a teenager. She felt good—wonderful. No, glorious, more vibrantly alive than she had ever felt before. "And I'm escaping into the shower," she went on in sudden inspiration. "You won't catch me, Copper."

Cameron burst into the room like a member of a SWAT team on a raid, immediately assuming the position, legs apart, knees slightly bent, arms extended straight out in front of him, hands clasped, as if around the butt of a revolver.

Sandra's expression of wide-eyed surprise was unfeigned; Cameron's appearance, buck naked, in that familiar stance, was more than surprising, it was flat-out hilarious. She clapped a hand over her lips to contain her laughter.

"Don't move, lady," he ordered, in a low, menacing voice. "I've got you covered."

"Not yet," she responded, laughing through her spread fingers. "But I do have hopes in that regard."

Cameron's blue eyes glittered with sheer devilment. "I'm afraid I'm going to have to take you into protective custody." He indicated the bathroom with a quick movement of his head. "In there, lady."

"Whatever you say, Officer." Tossing aside the nightshirt she'd pulled from a drawer along with her robe, which she'd been holding in front of her nude body, Sandra started toward the bathroom in a sashaying stroll. Glancing back over her shoulder, she gave him a smoldering look and a throaty invitation. "Walk this way."

"Well, if you insist," he said doubtfully. "But I'm going to look pretty silly." Lowering his arms, he straightened and crossed the room to her, mimicking her hip-swaying stroll.

Sandra lost it.

So did Cameron.

Roaring in laughter, he swept her up into his arms and carried her into the bathroom, there to indulge in what she would later decide was probably the longest shower on record, possibly in history.

She reveled in every minute of it.

"That was wonderful." Sandra patted her lips with a paper napkin, then dropped it onto her empty plate.

Several hours had elapsed since their shower-lovemaking marathon. Long spears of late-afternoon sunlight lent a mellow glow to the room.

After an energy-restoring nap, they had dressed, picked up their clothing from the living room floor, unloaded and unpacked his gear, then headed for the kitchen for much-needed sustenance.

Cameron had insisted on preparing the repast.

"Thank you, ma'am. I aim to please." He grinned at her over the rim of his coffee cup.

"No, I'm serious," she said. "That western omelet was perfect, golden brown outside, creamy inside. You really are a very good cook."

"Thanks again," he said quietly, setting the cup on the table. "But I owe it all to my teacher."

Sandra's eyes widened in surprise. "You went to a cooking school?"

"No." Cameron shook his head, dislodging a lock of hair as golden brown as the omelet had been. "My teacher was a mother who firmly believed that being born a male did not excuse a child from lessons in the basics of domesticity." His quick, soft chuckle was threaded with loving remembrance. "She insisted that her sons be housebroken."

"Sons?" Sandra asked, suddenly realizing how very little she knew about him, this Lone Wolfe who was now her lover. "How many are there?"

"Four." He pushed back his chair and got up to walk to the countertop. Sliding the glass carafe from the heating plate of the coffeemaker, he returned to refill their cups. "I'm the eldest."

"Four sons," she murmured in awe, absently lifting her cup to take a careful sip of the hot liquid. "The mere thought of raising four boys is daunting."

Cameron laughed, and began collecting dishes and cutlery. "Believe me, it would have taken a lot more than us kids to daunt my mother."

Sounds formidable, Sandra mused—a veritable shining example of the traditional wife and mother, old-fashioned and outdated now, but fondly recalled, if Cameron's expression was anything to judge by. The total opposite of her own mother, she ruminated, rising to help him clear the table. Her mother had been a career woman to the oval tips of her fingernails. She'd been forced into an early retirement a few years ago, due to a heart condition—which, thankfully, was not life-threatening—and probably would have gone into a decline if faced with the very thought of taking on the role of housewife and mother to four children.

"At present, she's eagerly looking forward to whipping her grandchildren into shape."

Cameron's laconic remark ended Sandra's introspective reverie.

"How many grandchildren are there?" she asked, looking away from the flow of water churning the detergent into a mound of bubbles in the sink.

"None." He moved his shoulders in a light shrug, then grabbed a dish towel from a wall-mounted hook in readiness. "That's why she's so eager. But she believes that now, at long last, she has reason to hope." He took the dripping plate she handed him and applied the towel as if he were an old hand at the chore.

Sandra finished rinsing the second plate and frowned as she handed it to him. "Why?" She shook her head, confused. "I mean, why does your mother now believe there's reason to hope for grandchildren?"

"Because my youngest brother, Jake, is getting married in June." He laughed. "It's kinda funny. The lastborn of Maddy's sons will be the first one to marry."

"All four of you are still single?" The dishes done, she moved to wipe the table.

"Yes, at least for a little while yet." He tossed the damp towel adroitly onto the hook. "I may be reading it all wrong, but something tells me things are heating up between my other two brothers, Eric and Royce, and their respective ladies." He grinned at her; she felt the effects to the tingling soles of her bare feet. "I believe my mother's thinking along the same lines," he explained. "She sounded suspiciously smug when I talked to her early this morning."

"Do you talk to your mother often?" she asked, thinking about her twice-monthly, insubstantial telephone chats with her own mother.

"At least once a week." He paused, then shrugged. "When I can."

Sandra didn't require further explanation; she understood the demands of his profession.

"That's nice," she murmured, meaning it. But then she flashed a teasing smile at him. "You're a good and considerate son."

His own smile flashed; it had a wolfish look. "I'm good at a lot of things." Appearing deceptively lazy, he strolled to her. "Exciting things."

"Really?" Concealing a sizzling inner response behind an expression of wide-eyed innocence, Sandra watched with mounting anticipation as he closed in on her.

"Hmmm..." Cameron came to a halt with his chest just brushing her already tingling breasts. His eyes were dark, hooded, sultry. "You need more proof?"

"Much more proof and I'll probably die from intense ecstasy," she said breathlessly.

"Yeah, but, as the old saying claims," he whispered, slowly rubbing his chest against the hardening tips of her breasts, "what a way to go."

Sandra could barely breathe; she couldn't think of anything at all—except for the riot of erotic images seducing her mind and thoughts.

"Wanna go with me?" His voice was so low, she could hardly hear him, but still she understood, understood and responded, almost violently, to the sexy intonation in his voice.

"To...to the bed?" Silly question.

"The bed. The couch. The floor." He made a quick hand gesture. "The kitchen table."

She blinked. "I've never made love on a kitchen table. I've heard of it, of cour— Oh!" she softly exclaimed as he deposited her on top of the table.

"I'll be happy to expand your experience," he said, unfastening her jeans and tugging them down, over her hips. Within seconds, her jeans and panties were lying in a heap on the floor, and his jeans and briefs were bunched somewhere around his knees.

Sandra sucked in a breath as Cameron moved into position between her thighs; in comparison to his aroused body, the table didn't seem nearly as hard as it had moments before.

Bending over her, he tormented her into readiness for him with his body and his mouth.

Sandra moaned, deep in her throat, when his teeth gently raked her aching nipple and the tip of his manhood nudged against her mound.

Hot and moist, eager to again experience the thrill of feeling him inside her, filling her, Sandra raised her hips, inviting his possession.

There was an instant's pause, the rustle of clothes as he kicked free of his jeans, the sound of tearing foil, then a murmured curse from Cameron.

Reaching out, Sandra stroked his hips, his tautly muscled buttocks and thighs.

Cameron shuddered in response, then plunged, deep, straight to the core of her desire.

It was fast, and furious, and utterly satisfying. In unison, they cried out in joyous release.

The purple shadows of encroaching evening dimmed the interior of the cabin as Cameron gently cradled Sandra in his arms and carried her into the bedroom.

Pearly pink dawn revealed a tangle of bedclothes and bodies sprawled across the bed.

The softly creeping light bathed Cameron's face, waking him. In turn, he woke Sandra with a creeping series of soft kisses, to her face and neck and breasts.

She stirred, stretched, and languidly wound her arms around his neck.

"You missed my mouth," she scolded, pouting.

"You're right," he agreed, kissing his way to her lips. "I missed it all night."

His morning kiss was cool, gentle, heart-wrenchingly tender. A warm moisture stung her eyes.

"That was lovely," she murmured on a sigh when he raised his head to gaze into her misty eyes.

"And so are you," he said, swooping to brush his lips over her sparkling wet lashes. "I could continue kissing you all day..." He lifted his head again, and gave her a teasing smile. "But you'd soon get tired of the growling demand for food from my stomach."

Sandra smiled back at him. "Is this your way of telling me that you're hungry?"

"Famished." Startling her with the sudden swiftness of his movement, Cameron swept back the covers and literally leaped from the bed. "I'll cook," he offered, striding for the bathroom. "Why don't you go back to sleep until breakfast is ready?"

"Wait!" Her cry brought him to a stop, hand extended for the doorknob. "I'm slept out." Scrambling from the bed, she slanted a twinkling glance at him. "Besides, I'd much rather shower with you."

His eyes narrowed suspiciously. "I'm not sure I can trust you. Do you promise to be good?"

Her smile mirrored the one he had given her in the kitchen last evening.

"I promise to be terrific."

Laughing and kissing, Sandra and Cameron lathered, and bathed, and satisfied each other's bodies.

Cameron cooked steaks on the outside grill for breakfast. Firmly refusing to even consider fat and calorie content, Sandra prepared fried potatoes and scrambled eggs on the side.

The meal was every bit as satisfying as their romp in the shower, if in a different manner.

After the meal was finished and the dishes were cleared away, they donned jackets and hiking boots and left the cabin to explore the terrain surrounding the building nestled in the foothills.

Their laughter ringing on the crisp spring air, they trudged hand in hand, stepping with care on the squishy ground and the patches of lingering snow along a steep mountain trail.

The outing was both exhilarating and exhausting. Sandra was panting from the exertion when they returned to the cabin.

"Time for lunch," Cameron said, after making a trip into the bedroom to hang up their jackets.

"Past time." She glanced pointedly at the clock; it read 1:45.

"And then a nap?" He leered at her.

"You're insatiable!" Laughing, she went to the cabinet to take out a can of soup.

"Hungry, too," he drawled, turning to the fridge. "You want a sandwich with your soup?"

And that was how the following days played out, slowly unwinding in an atmosphere of domestic tranquillity and sensuous bliss.

On Saturday evening, happy and content with each other, Sandra and Cameron decided to make a celebration of their first week together.

Sandra donned the two-piece confection her parents had sent her from Paris for her birthday; Cameron dressed casually but elegantly in brushed-denim pants and a crisp white silk shirt. The effect of their sartorial efforts on one another was immediate appreciation.

Seated opposite one another at the dinner table, they devoured each other with their eyes, while devouring grilled salmon, crisp salad, and the pale gold wine Cameron had brought with him.

Later that night, all her appetites sated, Sandra lay curled against Cameron's warmth, awake while he slept, musing on the sweet satisfaction of two individuals in seemingly perfect harmony.

Maybe, she thought muzzily, floating in the nether area between sleep and wakefulness, just maybe, there really could be such a thing as an equal, balanced, happy and mutually satisfying marriage between two independent, career-minded people.

She floated off to sleep in a contemplative bubble of contentment.

As all bubbles eventually do, Sandra's burst. The deflating pinprick came early Sunday morning, in the form of a summons from Cameron's beeper. The muted beep penetrated her unconsciousness; the noise Cameron made fumbling with the bedside phone drew her to the surface; the sound of his voice brought her to awareness.

"It's Wolfe. What's up?"

Well I am, for one, Sandra grumbled to herself, shifting into an upright position in the bed.

"When?"

When what? she asked herself, covering a yawn with the palm of her hand. And what was so all-fired important that it warranted a call at this time of the morning?

"Damn it all to hell!"

She blinked. Whatever the call was about, from the tone of Cameron's voice, it sounded serious.

"Okay, thanks, Steve." He heaved a sigh. "Yeah, I'll be careful."

Careful? About what? Or whom? Her curiosity aroused, Sandra watched as he replaced the receiver and sat still for a moment, staring into space. His very stillness sent an apprehensive shiver down her spine.

"Cameron, is something wrong?"

He heaved another sigh before turning to her; the look of him intensified the shiver.

"What is it?" she asked, impulsively reaching a hand out to him.

"*It* is a man," he said, curling his hand around hers. "And it means the end of our time here together."

Sandra's spirits did a swan dive. Her hand tightened on his. "You must leave?"

"Yes." His voice was flat, which said a lot about his spirits.

"Work-related?" Sandra knew better than to ask for anything other than the bare essentials.

"Yeah."

She nodded in acceptance, expecting no further explanation, but he surprised her with his willingness to be more forthcoming.

"While you were waging your custody battle in court I was chasing a two-bit bank robber turned kidnapper and rapist." The shadow of a wry smile flickered briefly on his lips. "I caught him, too." He jerked his head to indicate the phone. "That call was from another agent, informing me that the

felon escaped from the lockup where he was await-
ing trial.''

"And the Bureau wants you to suspend your vacation to track him down?''

"No." Cameron shook his head. "That call
wasn't official. But the agent thought I should
know about the situation, since the felon had sworn
to track me down if he ever gained his freedom.''

"But . . . I don't understand.'' Sandra frowned.
"I mean, we're secluded here. This man, this felon,
can't possibly know you're here. Why would you
leave and put yourself in harm's way?''

"I have a duty, a responsibility to—''

"Your responsibility in this instance is to yourself,'' she said, interrupting him. "What are you
thinking of doing—making yourself a sitting duck,
using yourself as live bait to lure the criminal?''

A smile flittered over his lips again. "Something
like that,'' he admitted.

"That's nuts!''

"Perhaps, but—''

"Cameron! Will you listen to yourself? Surely
you don't believe you're the only agent capable of
capturing this . . . this outlaw?''

"No, of course not,'' he immediately replied.
"And I wasn't thinking of playing the macho hero
and going after him alone. But I should be part of
the team.''

"Why?" she demanded, fearful for his safety, and incensed by his adamancy. "I could accept your attitude if the call had come from your superior, ordering or even requesting your help, but your deciding to use yourself as bait doesn't make sense."

This time he didn't smile; he grinned.

"What's so funny?" she asked suspiciously.

"You." He gave her hand a quick squeeze. "You sound just like a prosecuting attorney grilling an unfriendly witness."

She gave him a dry look. "I was trained to apply logic, and reason, and good old-fashioned common sense, you know."

"And you apply it to advantage."

Sandra's spirits surfaced from the depths into the sunshine. "You'll stay?" She didn't try to contain the breathless, hopeful note in her voice.

"Yes." He nodded, then quickly cautioned her, "At least for a day or so, until I hear how the hunt is progressing. But if it turns out that they could use me..." He let his voice trail away.

"I understand." Giving his hand a final squeeze, she slipped away from his hold and left the bed.

"Where are you going? It's still early—why not catch a little more sleep?"

"I'm awake now," she said, heading for the bathroom. "And I'm hungry."

"Yeah, well, so am I." He grinned suggestively. "That's why I wanted to stay in bed."

"Guess you'll have to settle for pancakes."

Laughing, Cameron leaped from the bed and tracked her into the bathroom.

Five

It began raining early Sunday afternoon, a gentle spring rain—or at least that was what Sandra and Cameron believed it to be.

Sometime during the night, after they fell asleep, the temperature took a sudden plunge and the rain turned first to sleet, then to ice.

They awoke Monday morning to an unnatural stillness outside, and an eerie grayish-white light seeping into the cabin.

"Snow?" Cameron guessed, padding barefoot and naked to the window.

"Possible," Sandra mumbled, burrowing deeper under the covers; she had experienced many Colorado spring blizzards.

"Not this time," he returned sourly, peering sleepy-eyed through the frost-rimmed pane. "We've got ice—boy, have we got ice."

"Ice?" Sandra repeated, tossing back the covers. Shivering, she came up behind him to stare over his shoulder. "Why, it's beautiful!" she exclaimed, entranced by the glistening coat weighing down tree branches, shimmering on the surface of their surroundings. "It's a winter wonderland out there."

"Yeah." Cameron sounded unconvinced. "The problem is, everything's frozen, and we're in the mountains."

"Oh, it is spring, you know," she said, dismissing his obvious concern. "It won't last long."

By midday, Sandra's assurances appeared prophetic. Although the sky was heavy with dark clouds, the distinct sound of melting ice rattled through the drainpipe from the roof, and small puddles of mud-swirled water dotted the driveway.

Braving the wet and slippery terrain underfoot, they ventured forth for a short walk, laughing as they took turns singing bits and pieces of "Slip Slidin' Away."

After dinner, content to be alone and quiet together, they didn't bother, or even think, to tune in to the radio or TV for a weather forecast, deciding it would be more interesting, and a lot more fun, to get comfortable on the floor in front of the crackling fire and play a few hands of strip poker.

Except for his shoes and socks, Cameron was still fully clothed while Sandra had lost to the tune of everything but her panties and bra, when his beeper once again shrilled an intrusion.

Sandra frowned to make clear her dissatisfaction with the annoying device.

"Duty calls, and all that," Cameron said, making an obvious effort to sound casual as he rose and sauntered into the kitchen to use the wall-mounted phone.

Suddenly cold, Sandra tugged the patchwork afghan from the couch and wrapped it around her chilled body.

Cameron stood facing her, and though she couldn't hear what he was saying, she could see his expression, and it was not an encouraging sight.

She read his lips when he bit out a socially unacceptable expletive. Then he turned his back to her, intensifying the chill permeating her being.

Hugging the soft wool throw to her shivering body, Sandra waited in dread for him to finish the call and return to her, certain the news was not good.

She was right. Still, he startled her with his first statement.

"You're going to have to leave here first thing tomorrow morning."

"Leave?" Sandra blinked. "Tomorrow? Why?"

"Because as long as you're with me, you are not safe." Cameron stood over her, scowling, and raked his fingers through his burnished hair. "That call was from the agent I talked to earlier. He told me that my apartment was broken into and ransacked this afternoon."

"And they believe it was that escaped criminal you told me about?"

"Yes. And they also believe he is tracking me."

Clutching the afghan, Sandra struggled to her feet to stand before him. "But then, why leave here? As I think I pointed out before, we're secluded here, and—" She paused when his hand sliced through the air, effectively cutting off her reasoned argument.

"And I'm afraid he knows exactly where we are," Cameron inserted, his voice heavy with disgust.

"That's ridiculous," she argued. "He's been in jail. How could he possibly know about Barbara's hideaway, or even me, for that matter?"

"So far as this place belonging to Barbara and you personally are concerned, he couldn't know," he readily agreed. "But he does know that I'm here. He knows, because I inadvertently told him."

"You told him!" Sandra cried, suddenly understanding that his obvious disgust was self-directed. "But how? You certainly couldn't have talked to him . . . could you?"

Cameron was shaking his head in denial before she had finished speaking. "No, I haven't talked to him. But what I did do was just as stupid." He heaved a sigh. "I left the written directions to the cabin lying in plain sight on my kitchen table."

"And your apartment was broken into and ransacked," she said flatly.

"Exactly."

"It's not going to require a lot of tracking ability on his part to find you, then, is it?"

He gave a quick, sharp nod. "Which is why I have got to get you out of here."

"But—"

He again cut her off. "At once." Pivoting, he started for the bedroom. "So I think you had better get busy packing."

"No." Sandra's soft but firm refusal brought him to an abrupt halt.

"No?" Cameron slowly turned to stare at her, his expression one of sheer disbelief.

"No." Sandra met his narrowed stare with cool composure, determined that she would not be panicked by the possibility of a criminal arriving on the scene. Nor would she tolerate being ordered about, not even by Special Agent Cameron Wolfe.

"What do you mean, *no?*" he asked, in a tone of controlled calm.

"I mean, no, I'm not leaving," she answered, in an equally calm tone. "I'm not afraid." That wasn't quite true. Still, while she felt a mite apprehensive about the situation, she felt an even deeper sense of anger and resentment at being summarily ordered to get packing.

Her calm demolished his calm.

"Dammit, woman, will you think?" He paced back to within a foot of her. "You're too bright to pull a childish rebellion act."

"Thank you... I think," Sandra said, maintaining her cool, while containing an impulse to slap him silly for the insult implied within the compliment. "Nevertheless, I won't change my mind." She arched her eyebrows. "Didn't you relay the same directions to this place to the agent you spoke to?"

"Certainly, but—"

"There you are, then," she said, coolly interrupting him. "Wouldn't you say that, even as we speak, there are any number of law enforcement officers, federal, state and local, converging on this place?"

"Probably, but—"

She interrupted him again. "I'd say definitely. So... not to worry. You may leave if you like, of course, to join your fellow officers in the chase, but

I...am...not...budging," she said, her firm tone emphasizing each word. "And don't call me 'woman.'"

Apparently rendered speechless, Cameron glared at her from glittering blue eyes, giving her the impression that at any moment smoke might well steam from his ears and nostrils.

Girding herself to withstand an onslaught of ranting and raving, Sandra clenched her muscles and drew her composure, along with the afghan, around her chilled and quaking body.

But Cameron didn't rant or rave. He heaved a deep sigh and gave her a knowing, cynical smile.

"I see. You're not pulling a childish act of rebellion at all, are you?" he observed, coolly and rather tiredly. "You're doing your in-your-face-and-be-damned ultrafeminist shtick. Right?"

Sheer rage swept through Sandra, a rage born of his blatant stupidity. How could he? she railed, literally shaking from the emotions roaring in protest inside her. After the days and nights they had shared, how could he dare to accuse her of now making an equal-rights stand? Didn't he know her primary concern was for him? His safety? And, if he didn't know, why didn't he know? Or why hadn't he at least asked?

So much for symbiosis and domestic harmony.

Sandra felt wounded, the pain running astonishingly deep. Freezing inside, she drew the mantle of hot fury around her.

"You're a fool, Wolfe," she said, concealing her pain with disdain. "And I can't be bothered sparring with fools."

Her budding hopes for their future killed by the frost of his cynicism, she gave him a dismissive once-over, then circled around him.

"Sandra?" There was a new, altogether unfamiliar and surprising note of uncertainty in his voice. "Where are you going?"

"To bed," she snapped, heading for the bedroom. "So if you're leaving, you'd better get your stuff together and out of the bedroom."

"I'm not going without you," he called after her, the note of uncertainty giving way to one of anger.

"Your choice." Sandra marched into the bedroom, tossed aside the afghan, pulled on her robe, then went to the linen closet to collect a quilt. Then, snatching his pillow from the bed, she marched back to the living room and threw the bedding at him.

"You're kidding." Cameron's eyes flashed blue fire at her; she deflected it with a cold smile.

"Laugh yourself to sleep." Swinging around, she strode from the room.

"Sandra!" He was right behind her—but a step and a half too late.

She turned the door lock an instant before he grasped the knob.

"Now you *are* being childish," he said, raising his voice to penetrate the barrier.

She didn't deign to answer.

"I won't beg," he threatened.

"I never thought you would."

"Are you going to open the door?"

"No." Sandra bit down on her lower lip, but she held her ground.

"Good night, Sandra."

Good night? Or goodbye? Tears rushed to her eyes, and she didn't trust her voice enough to respond. The tears spilled over onto her cheeks when she heard him sigh and move away.

Standing stock-still, Sandra glanced at the bed, then quickly glanced away. The standard-size double bed looked so big, so empty, so lonely. After the thrilling nights spent in that bed with Cameron, could she bear to even think of crawling into that bed alone?

All she had to do was unlock that door and call to him, for him, an inner voice whispered.

No. She shook her head. After the closeness, the intimacy, they had shared, he had misread her motives completely, accusing her of militancy, self-interest, when in fact her concern was all for him.

Suddenly impatient, with Cameron, with herself, she brushed the tears from her cheeks with a swipe of her hand. If he was too dense to discern that she felt she couldn't leave him to face the danger alone, that was his problem, not hers.

Shrugging out of her robe, her panties and bra, Sandra pulled on her nightgown and slipped into bed. She had slept alone before...for a good many years. Like it or not, she could sleep alone again.

She didn't like it. She didn't do much sleeping, anyway. Awake and miserable, she lay, stiff and tense, listening to the pinging sound of sleet striking against the windowpanes.

But, although she couldn't know it, Sandra wasn't the only one awake and miserable.

Cameron hadn't even bothered to lie down. He felt too restless, too agitated, too damn mad to lie still and quiet; the emotions roiling inside him wouldn't be contained, had to be released by some form of action.

The first of those actions was reflexive, second nature to him after his years with the Bureau. Shoving his bare feet into his running shoes, he left the house and made his way cautiously to his vehicle. Quickly retrieving his holstered gun, he spared a moment to rake the area with a narrow-eyed sweep before returning to the house, wet and shivering from the cold, sleet-spattered rain.

Spring.

Right.

Scattering cold droplets with an impatient shake of his head, he kicked off his shoes, then padded to the couch to slip the weapon beneath the end cushion. Still shivering, he moved to the fireplace and placed another piece of wood on the dwindling flames.

The fire blazed to renewed life, radiating heat and warmth. But the warmth didn't penetrate the surface of his skin, didn't touch the cold and empty spot deep inside him; only crawling into bed beside Sandra could have warmed him to the core of his being.

The realization of how very important she had become to him, to his physical and mental comfort, startled him, made him uneasy and even more restless.

Dammit, he cursed in silent frustration, venting his restlessness by prowling the room. What was with the woman? Oh, yeah, she had ordered him not to call her "woman," he savagely reminded himself, making a sharp turn into the kitchen.

But, hell, she was a woman—wasn't she? Oh, yeah, he answered himself. He knew firsthand, up close and personal, that Sandra was all woman.

All feminist woman, he recalled, making a sour face and a rude noise.

The very last thing he needed was to get hung up on a woman who wouldn't hesitate to whip out a little copy of her own personal Declaration of Independence every time she decided he was pulling a male-superiority act.

What kind of a masochistic idiot was he, anyway? he railed at himself, deliberately stoking his anger, to smother the disappointment and hurt he was feeling. How many times did he have to get emotionally raped by a woman before he got smart enough to keep his emotions inviolate?

And what in hell did he want in here, anyway? Cameron skimmed the nearly dark room with narrowed eyes, seeking diversion from his own thoughts.

Coffee. That was it—he needed some coffee.

He moved to the countertop—only to stand there, blankly staring at the automatic coffeemaker. What did he think he was doing? he chided himself. Coffee would only wire him, and he was strung too damn tight now.

Spinning around, he headed for the fridge; what he really needed was a beer, maybe several beers.

Cameron never finished the first can he opened; he was too busy pacing off a path in the rug to take the time to swig from the can.

Was Sandra asleep?

He groaned aloud. Damn. Why had he thought about her sleeping? Thinking about her, in bed, sleeping or awake, caused a yawning hollowness inside him, a yearning, sharp and deep, to be there, burrowed beneath the covers, beside her, inside her.

"Sandra."

Cameron froze, startled by the whispery longing in his own voice. Hell, he had it bad . . . whatever *it* was.

Love?

Remaining perfectly still, he examined the word that immediately sprang into his head.

Love?

He rolled the word around in his mind. He had been in love before, years ago. Yet it hadn't felt anything near like what he had experienced these past days with Sandra. Never before had he experienced the roller coaster of sensations and emotions he had felt simply from being with her. Over the past week, his feelings had run the gamut, from the highs of euphoria, possessiveness, protectiveness and happiness, to the lows of anger, anxiety, frustration and hopelessness miring him now.

But did those varied and confusing sensations and emotions equate to love . . . or were they the natural response to an appreciation of really great sex?

God. Cameron was developing a headache. All this probing of his psyche was getting to him.

And none of his internal dialogue had so much as touched on the cause of his present dilemma, that of his need to get Sandra out of the cabin and harm's way.

He sighed and raked a hand through his hair. She had stated adamantly that she would not budge. Furthermore, she had sounded as if she meant it. He was fresh out of ideas as to how to go about convincing her to leave, short of tossing her over his shoulder and physically removing her from the place.

Yeah. Right.

A grim smile played over his lips as he imagined himself playing Tarzan to her Jane.

Although it held sensuous appeal, he knew he could scratch that particular fancy.

Shaking his head in despair at his dearth of ideas, Cameron retraced his steps into the kitchen to set the half-full can of beer in the sink.

It was only then, standing so close to the window above the sink, that he became aware of the wind picking up speed, and what was now mostly sleet sweeping across the deck and against the pane.

Oh, hell. What was he racking his brain for? he thought irritably. From the sound of the wind and sleet, they were going to be iced in and unable to go anywhere, anyway. Might as well try to get some sleep.

Cameron did try. He just didn't succeed too well. The couch wasn't long enough for his tall frame, and the cushions suddenly felt lumpy. Besides, Sandra wasn't curled up next to him. And, in addition to the physical discomforts, the concept of love, romantic love, the forever-after concept of love, persisted in dancing around the fringes of his mind, tormenting him with the hopelessness of a man like him, already made wary of females, falling for a blazing feminist like Sandra.

How was a man to sleep under those conditions?

Had she reacted immaturely?

The question loomed ever larger throughout the dark hours in Sandra's alert consciousness.

When it first slithered into her head, she had made a snorting sound of rejection, then flipped from one side to the other in the seemingly too-roomy bed.

But the inner probe proved impervious to rejection, continuing its stabbing forays into her attention.

By somewhere around two-thirty or three, Sandra gave up evasive tactics. Flopping onto her back, she stared into middle distance, as if expecting an answer to magically materialize, written in bold letters against the darkness by a fiery finger of illumination.

And, to a certain extent, her expectations were realized. Dawn came to Sandra's consciousness hours before it grayed the eastern horizon.

Heaving a tired sigh, she bravely faced the truth: Of course she had reacted immaturely, simply because she had reacted emotionally instead of intellectually.

Women in love were known to do that occasionally—or so Sandra had always heard.

It was a bit of a shock. Sandra had never considered herself one of the typically portrayed helplessly emotion-driven females.

Love did really strange things to people—Sandra had heard that maxim more than once, as well.

And here she was, flat on her back in bed, staring into the darkness of the predawn house, vigorously engaged in an argument with herself.

Strange indeed.

The really hard-to-take part was, she was losing the damn argument!

Having always judged herself a thoughtful and rational being, capable of stepping around emotions to examine the cold, hard facts, both in her private and professional life, Sandra now felt challenged to live up to her own intellectual capabilities.

So then, had she reacted immaturely to Cameron's marching orders?

Of course she had.

Once she'd admitted the obvious, the emotional trigger was easily identified. In point of fact, Sandra acknowledged, she loved Cameron more than she valued her own physical safety and well-being.

But, naturally, she couldn't tell him that, Sandra realized with a sinking sensation. She very much feared that, should Cameron sense even a hint of her true feelings for him, he'd back away in an instant. He hadn't been tagged the Lone Wolfe by his contemporaries without reason. In a nutshell, despite the occasional indulgence of the senses, he preferred being alone.

By the time a weak and sickly light had somewhat brightened the room, Sandra had resolved her inner conflict. In essence, she would continue as she had begun, even if that meant maintaining to Cameron what he perceived as her position of immaturity and feminist militancy.

Resigned to the role, she pushed back the covers and dragged her tired body from the bed. She had little choice but to maintain her position, she reasoned. Because there was no way in hell she'd allow him to remove her to a safe place, then return to face the danger alone—even though he was trained and paid to do precisely that. Besides, there would very likely be the nearest thing to a platoon of law officers swarming around the cabin.

A woman's got to do what a woman's got to do. A wry smile flickered over her lips as Sandra repeated the catchphrase to herself.

Her smile fading, she pulled on her robe and pulled tight the belt around her waist, literally girding herself to approach the Lone Wolfe in the living room.

He wasn't there. Sandra found Cameron in the kitchen, sitting at the table, hunched over the cup of steaming coffee cradled in his hands.

"Good morning," she said, wincing at the tone she had deliberately hardened to conceal her trepidation.

"Oh, you're speaking to me again," he muttered, glancing up at her without raising his head. "You can afford to be gracious, I suppose, now that the weather has settled the issue of contention between us."

Weather? Sandra frowned and moved to gaze out the window above the sink.

"Oh!" she exclaimed in a surprised murmur.

The scene beyond the pane was again one of a winter wonderland, every surface locked in ice, glittering in the pale light of morning.

"Yeah," he said disgustedly. "Even if you agreed to go, I couldn't take you down that road. The Jeep's great in snow, but it don't do diddly on ice."

"But then . . ." Sandra swung around to look at him. "It works both ways, doesn't it?"

It was Cameron's turn to frown; he produced more of a beetle-browed scowl.

She rushed on. "I mean it stands to reason that if you can't get down the road, then that man, that criminal, can't get up the road, either." She fought to keep the note of triumph from her voice; she didn't quite succeed. "Isn't that right?"

"Sure," he readily agreed. Then he delivered the pinprick that burst her balloon. "That is, of course, unless he is already up here."

Sandra grimaced; she hadn't thought of that.

Six

The day dragged even more than the previous night, and was fraught with tension.

Cameron was moody and mostly silent, deflecting her few innocuous remarks with growled monosyllables, which in turn sparked a fire of anger and discontent inside Sandra.

At regular, almost predictable intervals, he prowled to the window to glare out at the road, as if willing the ice to melt from the heat of his angry stare.

Not only did the ice not melt, but by late afternoon the temperature had plummeted, ensuring that the frigid conditions would last through the coming night and into the morning.

And throughout the day, whenever a branch creaked from the weight of the ice, or a window rattled from the gusty wind, he went stock-still and alert, eyes narrowed, muscles taut, as if readying for action.

In those moments, he was more than unnerving; he was flat-out frightening.

While preparing dinner, Sandra surprised herself by suddenly wishing for a warming trend and thaw that would set her free from her confinement inside the cabin, even if it meant being hustled back to Denver.

Being caged with a restless, disgruntled Wolfe was not her idea of a relaxing vacation.

"What are you cooking?"

Though Sandra started, she managed to hold back a yelp of surprise at the unexpected and almost human sound of his voice so close behind her. Composing herself, she slowly turned to look at him.

"Snails and puppy-dog tails?" he went on, in a peacemaking, cajoling tone.

"I'm fresh out of those," she rejoined dryly. "You'll have to settle for meat loaf."

"I love meat loaf." He gave her a tentative smile; she didn't return it.

"Most men do." She turned back to peeling potatoes. "So do I," she said, leaving him under no illusions that she had chosen the meal to pacify him.

"You're really ticked, aren't you?"

"Me? Ticked?" She swung around again, this time brandishing the paring knife. "Why ever would you think that I'd be ticked?"

Eyeing her warily, Cameron took a satisfying step back. "Careful with that thing," he murmured in warning.

"This thing?" She held the knife aloft, relishing the moment as she examined it, before giving him a droll glance. "Afraid I'll peel you along with the potatoes?"

"Feel inclined to take a strip off my hide, do you?" Amusement laced his serious voice.

"I feel inclined to tell you to go—"

His beeper sounded, overriding her need to vent her anger and resentment. Frustrated, hating the damn beeper, and pretty close to hating him at the moment, she watched him stride into the living room to where he had left the dratted thing on an end table.

Swinging around, she rinsed the potato, quartered it, placed the pieces in the roast pan with the other chunks of potatoes, carrots, onions and celery arranged around the meat loaf, then shoved the pan into the oven.

When she turned again, Cameron was standing propped against the kitchen wall, his back to her, talking softly into the phone.

More trouble? she wondered, heaving a sigh. Not wishing to appear at all interested, she took off for the bedroom, to shower and change before dinner.

She lingered beneath the shower spray, half believing Cameron might join her there.

He didn't. Nor did he enter the room while she was dressing. Optimistically hoping his call had been good news—like the information that the escaped criminal had been apprehended, thereby allowing them to resolve their differences, if that was possible, and get on with their vacation, should they still be on speaking terms—Sandra left the bedroom with her fingers crossed.

After one look at Cameron's face as she entered the kitchen, Sandra uncrossed her fingers. So much for wishful thinking, she chided herself.

"Well?" she asked impatiently, when he was not immediately forthcoming.

"You can't go back to Denver."

Perplexed at hearing him state the obvious, Sandra stared at him a moment before replying, "I know, everything's covered with ice out there."

"Even if there were no ice, you couldn't go back."

"Why not?" she asked, in a reasonable tone that she hoped concealed the impatience gathering speed inside her.

"Whitfield's back in Denver." His taciturn response was, for Sandra, as good as no response at all.

"Back from where?" Her brow crinkled in a frown of utter confusion.

"Chicago."

That terse tidbit of information meant nothing to her; she hadn't even known Whitfield had left Denver, nor would she have cared if she had known.

"Uh-huh." Her hard-fought-for reasonable tone lost ground to advancing irritation. "I don't think we're connecting here. What, exactly, whether or not he's in Chicago, does Raymond Whitfield have to do with my returning to Denver?"

Cameron raked a hand through his hair, betraying his own fraying patience. "I think Whitfield was laying down a smoke screen by flying to Chicago."

Sandra literally threw up her hands. "Well, that explains everything." Controlling herself with effort, she took a quick breath, and tried again. "Cameron, I haven't a clue as to what you're talking about."

"Whitfield," he barked. "I put a surveillance team on him. He flew to Chicago last Saturday morning, but now he's back in Denver."

"So what?" she asked, more confused than before. "And why in heaven's name put a surveillance team on him in the first place?"

"Because of the threats he'd made to you, that's why," he said, a tone usually reserved for slow learners. A tone, moreover, that she rather resented.

"But that's ridiculous!" Sandra was barely hanging on to her temper. "I told you I thought Whitfield was only making noises."

"Oh, yeah?" His blue eyes glittered beneath raised golden brown brows. "Well, you thought wrong." He indicated the phone with a sharp head movement. "That call was to the operative I've got tailing Whitfield. He told me he followed Whitfield from the airport, straight to your apartment."

Though she managed not to show it, Sandra was a little shaken by the news. "Still, that doesn't mean he had anything sinister in mind," she said, unsure whether she was trying to convince him, or herself.

"It wouldn't, if he had gone about it in a normal way." Cameron shook his head. "But he didn't. He sat in his car until it was dark, then he poked around, not only at the front of the complex, but the back, as well. Then he returned to his car. He was still there, just sitting and watching the place, when the agent beeped me."

Really shaken, Sandra nevertheless put up a brave front. "That doesn't prove he means me harm," she said, hoping she was right, but fearing she wasn't.

"No, it doesn't, but—" he smiled in a feral way that raised the short hairs at her nape "—I'm not taking any chances, with either Whitfield or Slim."

"Slim?" She frowned, having momentarily forgotten the escapee his fellow agents were certain was tracking Cameron. "The criminal?"

"The same." Cameron paced to the window to peer into the darkness. Grunting, he flipped the switch that activated the trouble lights positioned at either corner of the house. "As soon as this damn ice melts, I'm getting you out of here."

Sandra had gone to the stove and pulled open the oven door to check their dinner. His flatly voiced statement made her pause as heat poured over her from the open oven. "Getting me out of here?" she repeated in sheer disbelief. "But you just a moment ago told me I can't go back to Denver."

He shook his head. "I meant that you can't go back to your apartment."

"I don't want to shock you," she said with sweet reason, "but my apartment is in Denver."

"Very funny." He grimaced. "But you know what I mean. I won't allow you to stay there alone.

Is there a friend you could stay with for a while? Maybe Barbara?''

"No." Sandra gave a quick, sharp shake of her head, deciding she had had enough. Allow her, indeed! Who did he think he was, her keeper? "Listen carefully, Cameron," she said distinctly. "I am not going anywhere. I am staying right here until I'm damn good and ready to leave. Now, have you got that?"

"Dammit, woman!"

"Stuff it, Wolfe," she retorted, turning to peer into the oven. "And I told you not to call me 'woman.'"

He was quiet while she spooned broth over the meat and vegetables. Ominously quiet, she thought, surprised that she didn't detect the scent of brimstone emanating from him. But the only scent assailing her nostrils was the mouth-watering aroma of roasting meat and vegetables wafting from the oven. When she slid the pan back on the rack, then shut the door, he heaved a sigh that held the unmistakable sound of defeat—if only in this round of their ongoing argument.

"How long until dinner is ready?" he asked, changing the subject. He inhaled, drawing in the tantalizing smell. "Do I have time to clean up?"

"Yes," she replied, striving for a neutral tone, grateful for the cessation of hostilities, however brief. "I figure it'll be another fifteen, twenty minutes." She shrugged. "Besides, it'll keep in a warm oven. Go have your shower."

"Right." Cameron took two steps, then paused to slant a faint but conciliatory smile at her. "How about breaking out the last bottle of cabernet? I think we both could do with a glass with dinner."

"All right," she agreed without hesitation, tentatively returning his smile.

He didn't move for a second, just stood there, staring at her. Then he nodded and strode from the room, leaving her to ponder on what he might be thinking.

Speculation ran swift and rife through her head. All sorts of unpalatable ideas came to mind.

It was now dark, heralding the approach of nighttime—bedtime. Was Cameron perhaps calculating his chances of later sharing the bed with her? Was he, by softening his voice and attitude, not to mention his request for wine, hoping to soften her, undermine her determination to remain steadfast to her principles?

Sandra loved Cameron. Although at this point in their relationship she was not prepared to admit that to him, she accepted it within her own mind and being. But loving did not blind her to the facts. She had been blessed by the sheer circumstance of birth with active intelligence, and expertly educated to dispassionately examine the facts of any matter or situation.

And so, by her very nature, she could not ignore or dismiss what she perceived as the facts in relation to her present circumstances.

The very fact that Sandra was now questioning Cameron's motives was telling, in and of itself. And what it was telling her was that she harbored grave doubts about placing her trust in him, and her heart with him.

This was a fact that did not bode well for any sort of meaningful relationship between them.

Accepting this fact was difficult for Sandra, perhaps the most difficult thing she had ever had to do. But there was no getting around it—although on a purely emotional level she longed to circumvent it.

No. Shaking her head, as if to free it of the doubts assailing her mind, she moved to busy herself setting the table for dinner.

Her dodging maneuvers were an abject failure; the doubts and questions persisted, stabbing into her mind, and thus her heart, with unrelenting reason.

Sandra had been interested in Cameron in a personal way since the moment she met him. More than interested, if the truth was faced—and in her case, it always was.

There had been between them an instant spark, a sensual recognition, a chemical reaction—whatever. She certainly had felt it; she had believed then, and believed even more strongly now, that he felt it, too.

It had been there from the first, a male-female thing, shimmering and crackling between them. That she had previously not indulged herself by exploring the intangible something had not altered or negated it. But, though she had not explored it, she had been receptive to every word spoken or murmured about the object of her interest. And the words she had heard over time about Cameron had not been encouraging.

Early on, Sandra had garnered the information that Cameron had been more than merely involved with a woman. That involvement, moreover, had progressed to speculation about an imminent announcement of their engagement. Then, abruptly, the speculation had ceased, replaced by an undercurrent of suggestion that the affair was over and, more to her interest, that Cameron had been left devastated by the perfidy of the woman, who had apparently dumped him for another, richer man.

Cameron had obviously been hurt in the process, and in turn, now she was feeling the pain.

Sandra sighed as she uncorked the wine to let it breathe.

Unbidden, she recalled hearing a scathing comment by a woman, somewhere, to the effect that the handsome and exciting special agent did not in fact like women, but merely tolerated them when the demands of sexual appetites had to be appeased.

At the time, Sandra had dismissed the remark out of hand as the nasty barb of a frustrated woman.

Now she wondered. And the very fact that she did so said much about her state of mind.

She had now spent over a week in Cameron's company. Day in, day out, to the exclusion of everything and everyone else, and at no time had she discerned so much as a hint indicating disdain for the opposite sex.

Quite the contrary. He had proved to be excellent and entertaining company, fun to be with, laugh with, make love with...especially to make love with.

But, of course, that was precisely what he had promised, wasn't it? Sandra reminded herself. Great sex. A sensual sabbatical.

And he had delivered, above and beyond the call, beyond her wildest imaginings.

Until the call to duty had intruded, dousing the fire of sensuality with the blanket of cold reality. And now it was over. She was in the way.

But there was still tonight to get through. And Cameron appeared prepared—no, eager—to suspend reality for one more night of sensual heat.

Sandra stared at the ruby red wine in the bottle, sniffed the intoxicating scent.

Did she want to play along, close her mind to the hopelessness of the situation, lose herself in the allure of his mouth, his touch, his possession?

Yes. Sandra wanted this night with him, more than she had ever before wanted anything.

Would she allow herself the license of mindlessness for the sake of one more night with him?

She hesitated . . . then closed her eyes against the pain of facing the bottom-line answer.

No.

She could not betray herself, any more than she could ever betray him.

She loved him. But a one-sided love was never, could never, be enough.

Sex was one thing. Love was another. And Sandra knew that for her, to hang on to one while denying the other would be self-destructive.

Her decision reached, she gathered her strength, steeled herself for the evening ahead.

But dreams, old and new alike, die very hard, and her mettle was tested with the first step Cameron took into the kitchen.

The look of him, showered, shaved, his damp hair appearing dark, like antique gold, stole her breath, and nearly shattered her resolve.

He was dressed in faded jeans that hugged his narrow hips and waist and delineated the musculature of his long legs. A stark white loose-knit sweater defined the width and breadth of his chest.

Swallowing a sigh of regret, while repressing a surge of desire for myriad things, physical and emotional, Sandra schooled her lips into a coolly remote smile.

"Dinner's ready," she said, in a hard-fought tone devoid of inflection.

He frowned, but said only, "Is there anything I can do to help?"

"You can pour the wine," she said, turning to open the oven door. "I'll bring the food."

Blaming the heat radiating from the oven for the sting in her eyes, Sandra mentally shored up her defenses, and grabbing pot holders, bent to the chore.

He had lost her.

Cameron had known it from the moment he walked into the kitchen endless hours ago.

It was late. He was tired. And he felt literally sick to his stomach. The feeling owed nothing to the delicious meal Sandra had prepared, or to the several glasses of wine he had consumed with the meal.

She hadn't even finished the first glass he had poured for her.

She had closed him out.

During the twenty or so minutes required for him to shower, shave and dress, Sandra had erected a barrier between them, an invisible yet impenetrable wall of resistance he had been unable to breach.

And Cameron had tried with every fiber of his being to tear down that barrier.

During dinner, and afterward, right up until she bade him a cool good-night, he had tried everything he could think of: conversation, humor, charm—what little he possessed—everything short of begging, to draw the warm woman from her cold shell of assumed indifference.

And Cameron believed Sandra's indifference was assumed; he had to believe it, because he couldn't bear to contemplate anything else.

Why?

What had he done wrong?

What terrible sin had he committed?

Why had she raised a shield against him?

Those tormenting questions were the direct cause of the roiling sensation sickening Cameron.

Twice. He had been rejected twice, and both times just as he was falling in love.

No.

Cameron shook his head. No. The first time hadn't felt anywhere near this painful. That had been nothing, *nothing,* compared to the sick sense of loss he was now suffering through.

And, try as he would, he could not convince himself that Sandra's sudden about-face had surfaced as a direct result of his accusing her of childishness and militant feminism.

No. It was more than that, deeper than that.

But... what?

Something in him.

The thought was unpalatable. Cameron didn't want to examine it, let alone accept it.

But there it was, entrenched in his consciousness, stabbing into his mind.

Something in him? Some essence, objectionable to the opposite sex, that he displayed?

Hell. Cameron raked stiff fingers through already wildly disheveled hair. He had had affairs with women other than the two he had unfortunately fallen for. And those other females hadn't shown signs of eventual objection to some offending essence within him.

In point of fact, it had been quite the contrary. More than one of those females had given unmistakable signals of desiring a deeper involvement with him.

So go figure.

Cameron moved his shoulders against his bed of sofa cushions in a half shrug. His advice to himself was excellent; too bad he couldn't follow it.

How in hell did a mere man proceed in figuring out the mind of a woman?

Talk to his mother?

Cameron was swept by an impulse to do just that. He immediately quashed the impulse with a self-taunting, *Get real, Wolfe.*

He was pushing forty, for Pete's sake, long past the age to solicit maternal advice on the proper course to steer on the rocky road to love. Besides, although he felt certain the indomitable Maddy would proffer the advice, his mother would likely laugh herself silly first. So scratch that idea.

His brothers? Hmm... That idea had merit. If he was reading the signs correctly, they appeared to be having little difficulty with the opposite sex.

But, appearances were often deceptive, he mused. Of course, there was a way of ascertaining the answer. He could call, perhaps even seek advice from one, or all three, of his brothers.

Then again, perhaps not. Cameron grimaced. Not only would he tarnish his image as the older and wiser, if somewhat aloof, mentor to the younger trio, but knowing them they'd probably laugh even harder than their mother.

He was fresh out of ideas, overtired, half-asleep, and vulnerable.

Cameron groaned in protest as an image formed to tease and torment his weary mind.

Sandra. She of the sable hair and laughing dark eyes. She of the keen intellect and riposte. She of the cool demeanor and hot mouth. She of the sleek body and long, libido-enticing legs.

"Stop." His hoarse, whispered plea froze in the cold night air and echoed inside his head.

Please, stop, he repeated in silent supplication to his own consciousness.

He was getting punchy from lack of rest, he mused muzzily, encroaching sleep sending his thoughts drifting along another track.

He yawned, giving in to the heavy weight dragging down his eyelids.

How were his siblings faring in their relationships with their respective ladyloves?

Seven

———

A violent late-spring thunderstorm from the west pushed over the mountains of northeastern Pennsylvania.

Sergeant Royce Wolfe barely heard the rapid swish of the sweeping windshield wipers. Hands steady on the steering wheel, he scanned the road with alert, experienced eyes. He had gone off duty a short time ago, but he was a law-enforcement officer, on or off duty.

Lightning streaked the midnight sky, bathing the surrounding mountainous terrain in an eerie glow for a flashing second. Thunder roared overhead, shaking the earth below.

Memory stirred inside Royce's mind. It had been just such a night as this, over a month ago, the first time he saw Megan.

There were differences. Important differences. A smile relieved the taut watchfulness of his ruggedly attractive features, eased the tension bunching his square jawline.

Oh, yeah. The differences were important. While maintaining his keen observation of the undulating road ahead, Royce gave memory free rein.

It had been storming that night, too, an early-spring storm, cold and sleety, the last gasp of an unrelenting winter.

He had first seen Megan Delaney slumped over the steering wheel of the sports car she had totalled running head-on into a highway guardrail.

Being off duty, but wanting to assist the patrolman who arrived on the scene minutes later, Royce had offered to follow the ambulance into town to secure a statement for the record from the accident victim after she regained consciousness.

That act of accommodation to a fellow Pennsylvania State Police officer had been Royce's undoing—and, eventually, the making of him.

Megan. His beautiful Megan, of the fiery hair, and the temperament to match.

She had hit that guardrail not entirely because she was driving too fast in inclement weather, as he had at first assumed. No, although she had been driving too fast, she had been in a state of rage and hysteria, tearing away from the scene of a near-rape in the parking lot of a restaurant located in the foothills, along a desolate country road.

Megan had understandably been left emotionally scarred and wary of men, much to Royce's distress, since he had experienced an immediate attraction to her.

A soft chuckle shimmered on the humid air in the closed vehicle, as Royce recalled the inner battle he had fought against his desire for the injured woman.

But all had ended well, as Megan had cast off fear to rush in, literally—again totaling a brand-new car—to assist him in the apprehension of her attacker.

And now he was driving through another storm after working the late shift. Only this time he was not headed home to his apartment, but to Megan, the home of his heart and soul.

Every light in the house appeared to be lit, Royce noted as he pulled into the driveway. A tender smile curved his lips. Megan's need to keep the house fully lit after dark when she was alone was one of the few lingering aftermaths of her ordeal.

He left the car and strode to the door, and as he jabbed his finger into the doorbell his stomach rumbled in anticipation of the snack-meal he knew she had ready and waiting for him.

Megan answered the door wearing a big smile and a skimpy, figure-revealing silk nightie.

"How did you know it was me?" he scolded in a soft growl, stepping inside and hauling her into his arms.

"I peeked out the window, Officer," Megan confessed, curling her arms around his neck. "Now, are you going to pick a fight or kiss me?"

"Dumb question." Royce flashed a grin and lowered his head to capture her mouth with his.

The snack she had waiting for him was destined to wait a little longer.

Scooping her up in his strong arms, Royce carried her unerringly into her bedroom, without so much as a minute slip of his lips against hers.

Megan was more than ready for him—she was way ahead of him. With a flick of each ankle, her satin mules went clattering across the room, and with a tug and a flip of her arms, her nightie sailed into the air. Then she went to work undressing him.

His blood running hot and eager, Royce trembled in response to her deft fingers, which found other, even more exciting employment after his clothes littered the floor near her slippers.

Their loving started slow and sweet, with teasing, suggestive murmurs and enticing all-over kisses and caresses. But by the time they could no longer bear the exquisite torture and merged into one, their loving was hot and fast and thoroughly satisfying.

Later, his senses sated, Royce sat alone at the kitchen table, wolfing down the sandwich snack she had prepared, appeasing a more mundane appetite.

"Royce..." Megan said, entering the room after having a shower, and now decorously covered by an ankle-length robe in a rich dark green velour.

"Hmm?" he murmured around a bite from the thick roast beef and cheese sandwich.

"Have you been discussing me with your mother?" she asked, taking the chair opposite him at the table, and snitching one of his potato chips to nibble on.

"Yes, just the other day," he said after swallowing. "I told her about you, and how I love you until it hurts." He raised tawny gold eyebrows. "Why?"

"Because I received this in the mail today." Megan drew a large square white envelope from the sideboard and laid it next to his plate.

Royce didn't need to open it. He knew what it was. He flashed a grin. "Mom sent you an invitation to Jake and Sarah's wedding?"

"Yes, obviously." She gave him an amused look. "Did you ask her to send it?"

"No." He shook his head.

Her expression sobered. "You don't want me to accompany you?"

"Get real, beautiful," he said, laughing. "You didn't need an invitation. I was planning on taking you with me, anyway."

"Oh, I see." Though her voice was cool, her relief was visible. "And when were you planning to tell me?"

"Tonight. Tomorrow." He shrugged. "Plenty of time. It's still over two weeks until the wedding."

Shaking her head in despair of men in general, and him in particular, Megan placed the half-nibbled chip on her plate.

Royce noticed. But then, he noticed just about everything concerning Megan. And she had always joined him in the late snack.

"Aren't you hungry?"

"I thought I was." She frowned and placed a hand over her stomach. "But I've been feeling a little queasy every time I eat the last few days. I think I might have a touch of a stomach virus."

"Have you been to see Virginia Hawk?" he asked with quick concern, referring to the doctor who had treated Megan after the attack and the subsequent accident.

"No, of course not," Megan replied, dismissing the very idea with a flick of one hand. "I'm not sick. I'm not running so much as a low-grade fever. I feel certain that it's simply a spring virus."

"But suppose it isn't?" he persisted. "Suppose it's an aftereffect of the trauma you suffered, evolving into a stomach disorder?"

"Royce, I'm sure it is nothing of—"

"But you can't be sure." He rose to circle the table to her and draw her up into the warm protection of his embrace. "What if you're wrong, and it's something more than a virus? If you're ill, and can't travel to Sprucewood with me for the wedding, I won't go, either. I won't go anywhere without you, ever again."

"Oh, Royce." Megan's eyes were suspiciously misty; her voice was roughened by emotion. "I don't ever again want to go anywhere without you, either, but I'm sure you're worrying without reason." She sniffed and offered him a tremulous smile. "I'll be fine, you'll see, and as you pointed out a moment ago, it's still over two weeks until the wedding. Please don't worry."

"I can't help but worry about you," he murmured, stroking one long finger down her cheek, to the corner of her mouth. "I love you so much."

"I know, and I love you." Megan kissed the tip of the finger he drew along her lower lip. "That's why I didn't want you to know about this dratted virus."

"Will you promise me something?" he whispered, replacing his arousing finger with his even more arousing mouth. "Will you promise to see

Doc Hawk if the symptoms haven't gone away within the next couple of days?"

"Yes, if you'll promise me something," she murmured against his teasing mouth.

"Anything. Name it." His tongue caressed her soft, parted lips.

"Promise you'll take me to bed within the next couple of minutes."

Laughing, Royce swept Megan up into his arms.

The second in the cluster of thunderstorms moving from west to east broke with a series of lightning cracks and resounding booms over Philadelphia shortly before six o'clock Monday morning.

The noise didn't wake Eric Wolfe; he had awakened some minutes before the storm hit. Propped up in the king-size bed in his apartment overlooking the Philadelphia Art Museum and the Schuylkill River, he had a panoramic view through the wide, west-facing plate-glass bedroom window of nature's violent display of breathtaking power.

But it wasn't violent or powerful enough to command Eric's exclusive attention. Every few seconds, his alert, expectant gaze sliced to the closed bathroom door.

It had been mere minutes, and yet the waiting was beginning to get to him.

Was she . . . or wasn't she?

When at last the door opened, he was caught unprepared, staring in wonder at a particularly long, seemingly horizontal streak of lightning.

"Eric."

The combined threads of trepidation and excitement woven through Tina's soft voice brought his head whipping around, his dark blue eyes probing hers.

Lord! How he loved this woman, this woman who had single-handedly healed the bitterness he had lived with after the death in the line of duty of his policeman father, thus freeing him to be a better, more effective undercover narcotics cop himself, this woman he had once suspected of having dealings with some low-life characters who were dealing in illegal substances.

But Tina Kranas had proved herself, her innocence, to his satisfaction long before she came to his defense by flying at the real guilty party—who happened to be her former husband—with a cast-iron frying pan.

"Well?" he prompted, then held his breath.

"It shows positive," she answered, holding aloft a home pregnancy strip. "It appears you are going to be a father."

"Hot damn!" Eric whooped, bolting from the bed and striding to her to catch her up in his arms. His immediate response chased the trepidation

from Tina's eyes, leaving them shining with pleasure.

"I've gotta call Mom," he said, planting a quick
kiss on her smiling mouth before releasing her to go
to the phone on the bedside table.

"Now?" Tina laughed. "Eric, it's not even seven
yet. You'll wake her."

"I know." He shot a grin at her, then continued
to punch in the number. "I know, as well, that
Mom would see me drawn and quartered if I didn't
tell her at once."

The phone in his childhood home in the small
town of Sprucewood, located some fifteen or so
miles outside Philadelphia, was picked up on the
third ring.

"Hello?" There was an underlying note in
Maddy Wolfe's voice that only her four sons would
have recognized and identified as fear of bad news.
It was a note familiar to the families of most dedi-
cated law-enforcement officers.

"It's me, Mom, and there's nothing wrong,"
Eric assured her at once, motioning Tina to his side
and curling an arm around her waist. "In fact, it's
very good news, news you've been waiting to hear."

"To use an over-used, trite phrase—" Maddy's
voice had resumed its normal, wry tenor "—I'm all
ears, son."

"Well, first I'd like your opinion on an idea I
have." His eyes gleamed with a teasing light that

was very familiar to Tina... and that would have been very familiar to the older woman, had she seen it.

"Get on with it, Eric." Now her voice held a warning that drew an appreciative chuckle from him.

"Right. Ah, how do you think Jake and Sarah might take to the idea of a double wedding?"

There was a brief pause, a breathless silence, and then: "Are you serious?"

"Oh, yeah," Eric said, tightening his arm possessively and protectively around Tina and gliding an adoring look over her glowing face. "Tina's pregnant, Mom. She just did the home test." Unable to contain the excitement bubbling inside him, he grinned again. "Metaphorically speaking, the rabbit died."

"You don't sound too despondent," Maddy observed, probing gently, hopefully.

"I'm over the moon," he said jubilantly. "We both are. It's no accident, you know. We were trying." His voice held laughter. "Trying hard."

"Before marriage?" A tiny note of censure there.

"Aw, Mom," he said, in the exact same tone he had used as a boy. "So what do you think—will Jake and Sarah go for it? We could kill two birds with one stone... so to speak."

"Or two Wolfes with one shotgun... so to speak," she retorted dryly.

It took a moment for the dawn to break in Eric's mind; Maddy waited with maternal patience.

"Sarah's pregnant!"

"Hmm..." she concurred in a murmur. "They told me just last night. I knew I had raised rambunctious sons. I just never realized quite how rambunctious."

Eric roared. "Is Jake happy about it?" he asked when his laughter subsided.

"To quote your youngest brother exactly," she drawled, " 'Is Elijah Blue?' "

Eric laughed again, then said, "I'll give Jake a call in a little while."

"You do that," Maddy replied. "And, Eric—"

"Yes, Mother?"

"Congratulations, son, and give my love to Tina."

"Thanks, Mom, I will."

Eric didn't replace the receiver after saying goodbye, but merely depressed the disconnect button, then moved his index finger to punch in the Sprucewood number registered to his younger brother, Jake. His intent was thwarted by Tina sliding her palm over the buttons.

"That can wait awhile," she said decisively. "At least until after breakfast."

"You're hungry?" Eric asked hopefully, somewhat surprised, since she'd been off her appetite the last week or so. At her nod, he dropped the receiver onto the cradle. "Good. I'll rustle up some eggs."

"No," she said, as he started to move, his encircling arm moving her along with him, toward the kitchen. "I'm not hungry for scrambled eggs."

He looked at her askance. "I hope you're not about to tell me you want pickles and ice cream."

"Don't be silly," Tina said. "No. What I want—must have—is chicken noodle soup."

"Chicken noodle soup!" Eric made a face. "At six-thirty in the morning?"

"*Eric,* please . . ." She batted her naturally long eyelashes exaggeratedly at him. "I'm eating for two now, you know. I need hearty sustenance."

He fought a grin, but it defeated him. "Okay, I give up," he agreed, releasing his hold on her and ushering her into the kitchen. "Chicken noodle soup it is."

"And toast bread."

"And toast." Silent laughter laced his voice.

"And a cinnamon bun."

Eric lost it; his laughter brightened the storm-dimmed room.

Thunder growled in the distance, rumbling a warning of the approach of the third storm in the clustered front moving rapidly from west to east.

A bemused smile tilting his lips, Jake Wolfe hung up the phone. He had been minutes away from leaving the split-level house he and Sarah had made settlement on two weeks ago, and into which he had moved the very next day, when the call came in from his brother Eric.

Imagine that, Jake mused, staring at the now silent instrument. Eric and Tina requesting they make the upcoming nuptials a double affair.

And Tina was also pregnant.

What a hoot! He couldn't wait to tell Sarah.

Sarah! Jake shot a glance at his watch, then shot down the three steps into the family room, then through the door connecting the house to the garage; if he didn't get his rump in gear, he'd be late.

He was supposed to pick up Sarah to deliver her to Sprucewood College in time to conduct her first class, and he had exactly five minutes to get there.

Fortunately, Sprucewood was a small town, and even more fortunately, the worst of the morning rush was over. Raindrops began pattering on the car roof as he turned onto Sarah's street.

She was waiting for him on the apartment's front steps, huddled beneath a small umbrella, the toe of one foot beating an impatient tattoo on the cement. She made a dash for the car as he glided to a stop alongside the curb.

"I was beginning to think you weren't coming, and that I'd be late to class," she gently scolded, sliding onto the seat beside him. "What kept you?"

"Wait till you hear," he said, breaking off for a moment to allow the laughter tickling his throat to escape. "You're gonna love it."

As usually happened, the rich, full sound of his laughter brought a delighted smile to her eyes and mouth. "I can't wait," she said in a teasing voice. "So, suppose you tell me."

"I had a phone call from Eric, that's what kept me," he began, pausing for another chuckle. "Damned if the clown doesn't want to get married with us."

Sarah blinked. Then she frowned her incomprehension. "What?"

"Do you remember I mentioned that Mom told me Eric had brought a young woman home to meet her, not just once, but twice?" he asked, then rushed on without giving her time to respond. "And that her name was Tina, and she was very nice, and that she baked lemon meringue pie almost as good as Mom's own?"

"Yes, of course I remember," Sarah answered when he finally paused to breathe. "How could I forget, when you made such a big deal out of it?"

"Knowing Eric, it was a big deal." Jake grinned. "Well, seems the ol' love bug's taken a big bite outta Eric's heart, and he and Tina wanted to know if you and I would consider a double wedding ceremony."

"Why, that's a wonderful idea!" Sarah exclaimed. "I hope you agreed."

"No." Jake gave a quick shake of his head.

"Why not?" Sarah frowned, and sent a quick glance to her watch.

"I wouldn't agree without talking to you first," he said. "You should know that."

"Thank you." Her smile was gentle, but fleeting. "I've got to go, or I'll be late." She groped for the release and swung the door open.

"But I didn't tell you the best part," he objected. "Eric and—"

She silenced him with a kiss, and then she slid across the seat and out of the car.

"It'll have to wait until lunchtime," she said, pressing the button to open the umbrella. "And if you don't get moving, you'll be late. Bye. Love you." She took off at a near-run along the campus walk."

"Sarah, slow down!" Jake called after her in sharp concern.

She flashed a grin at him over her shoulder, adjusting her pace to a brisk, striding gait.

Jake anxiously watched her until she entered the building. Then he set the car in motion to wend his way to the station.

After reporting in, he got behind the wheel of his black-and-white police cruiser and began his regular routine of patrol.

Jake loved being a cop, enjoyed waving to and exchanging friendly gibes with kids of incremental ages as he patrolled the area around the elementary, middle and high school. From there, his route took him around the outer boundaries of the college.

But even after seven months he still could not drive the college perimeters without recalling the events of the previous autumn.

That was when Jake had first met, and been immediately attracted to, Sarah Cummings.

Now he could reflect gratefully on the incident, for it had inadvertently brought him and Sarah together. But at the time, the mystery of Sarah had nearly driven him to distraction.

The incident had involved the crime of car theft, or more precisely car-parts theft, undertaken by three upper-middle-class college students on a whim, just to see if they could get away with it.

And they might have, Jake conceded, had it not been for the threat posed by Sarah to the three of them, because she had accidentally overheard them discussing their nefarious activities, and his subsequent interest in her.

Oh, it had stumped him for a while, the glaring fact that she shied away from being seen in public with him, especially when he was in uniform.

But Jake had eventually worked it all out, then set about catching the young men with the goods—

with Sarah's help, he admitted, smiling at the memory of her wielding a stout branch to knock a tire iron meant for his head out of the hand of the self-appointed leader of the three.

Savoring the warm memory of his beautiful Sarah rushing to his defense, Jake happily continued his patrol, stopping occasionally, chatting with friends and acquaintances, until it was time to meet Sarah for lunch.

She was waiting for him in their usual back booth in the off-campus hamburger joint where he had first spotted her seven months ago. She was wearing the same big round tortoiseshell glasses that gave her a wide-eyed, owlish appearance.

The sight of her softened and hardened Jake at one and the same time.

"Hi," he murmured, sliding onto the bench opposite her in the booth, slightly awed and amazed at the ever-deepening love he felt for her.

"Hi." Sarah returned his greeting, the glow in her eyes proof that she returned his love in equal measure.

"Got time to hear about Eric now?"

"I'm all yours for exactly fifty-five minutes," she said brightly.

"You better be—for fifty-five minutes, and forever," he growled.

"Eric?" She laughed and arched her eyebrows.

"Yeah." He grinned. "He and Tina are pregnant, just like you and me."

"I think it's wonderful."

"So do they." He laughed and shook his head. "And you really don't mind making it a double wedding?"

"Not at all. It'll be fun." Her eyes danced with amusement. "And your mother will love it."

"According to Eric, she already does." Jake erupted in laughter as another consideration sprang to mind. "And I can't wait to hear what Cameron will have to say. Two weddings *and* two babies! He'll freak..."

Eight

Cameron woke to the sound of running water, both inside and outside the house. Frowning, he pried his eyes open to a slit and peered at the face of his watch. The position of the hands brought his eyes wide open.

Twelve-fourteen! He never slept so late—except on days when he didn't get to sleep until dawn. And this was, had been, one of those days, or nights, or whatever.

The sound of water running inside the house ceased abruptly. The running outside continued, but sounded faint and distant. But, as faint and distant as the sound was, it activated a sudden realization in the sleep-fogged depths of his mind.

The ice was melting, which could only mean that the capricious spring weather had once again turned seasonally mild. Which, in turn, meant that he and Sandra were no longer confined to the cabin.

Which also meant it was time, past time, to haul his carcass off the sofa.

Stifling a groan at a protest of his stiff and cramped muscles, aching from his six-foot-four-inch frame being confined to a six-foot area of space, Cameron levered himself into a sitting position.

Upright, and almost fully conscious, Cameron inhaled, and stifled another groan, this time in appreciation of the aroma of fresh coffee wafting from the kitchen, which explained the source of the previous sound of running water inside the house.

His nose twitched and his mouth watered as the aroma got stronger, seemed nearer.

"Good morning." Sandra's voice was utterly devoid of inflection, good, bad or indifferent.

But there wasn't a thing indifferent about the sensations that ripped through him when he glanced up at her. She appeared so feminine, so soft and sleek in her robe and slippers, that he longed to reach out and draw her into his arms, bear her down with him, onto the couch, and make love to her, with her, until they both forgot what had caused the friction between them.

Prudence cautioned him against fulfilling the longing; prudence, and the closed look of her.

"Good morning," he returned, wrapping his hands around the heated mug. "And thanks."

"You're welcome." She didn't smile; she turned away. "I'm poaching eggs. They'll be done in a few minutes . . . if you want some."

"Yes, I want some," he said to her retreating back, careful not to slosh the coffee as he stood up.

"Then come butter the toast."

Her tone—or rather the lack of it—didn't bode well for a comfortable, congenial meal, Cameron reflected dejectedly, trailing her into the kitchen.

His reflection proved correct.

Seated opposite her at the table, Cameron acknowledged that the three or so feet of space separating them was as good as a mile.

Sandra wasn't picky, or argumentative, or downright bitchy. What she was, in his view, was much worse. She was remote, withdrawn and—he shuddered at the thought—lost to him.

She deflected with a look, a frown, a raised eyebrow, every attempt he made, hapless as he knew it to be, to ease the tension between them.

He was beginning to feel desperate by the time he finished the two perfectly cooked poached eggs she had silently served him.

The very last thing Cameron needed at that point was the intrusive sound of his beeper.

So, of course, the way his luck had been running lately, that was exactly what he got.

Sandra briefly lost her rigidly controlled expression to a cynical smile.

Cameron had to quash an urgent impulse to hurl the blasted beeper through the window.

But the very fact that he had felt the impulse was both startling and edifying.

Cameron identified the root cause of his uncharacteristic feeling as he dutifully responded to the call of duty; in simple terms, Sandra had become more important to him than his life's work.

From the unreachable depths of her silent withdrawal, she monitored his every reluctant step to the kitchen wall phone. Then, as he reached for the receiver, she stood and walked out of the room.

"When you're finished on the phone, you can clear the table." Her remote voice floated back to him. "I'm going to dress."

Damn.

Fighting the desire to desert his post and go after her, Cameron punched in the designated number.

"Wolfe. What's up?" he snapped, the instant the receiver was lifted at the other end.

"It appears our quarry slipped through the net," Steve's familiar voice replied, in unfamiliar tones of heavy disgust.

"How?" Cameron literally growled the demand for a plausible answer.

"He's a cunning son of a bitch," Steve said. "He kept moving in circles, then doubling back. Then he changed direction and made a run south. The local law lost him near the New Mexico state line. Seems friend Slim is heading home to Taos."

A conflicting wave combined of equal parts anger and relief washed over Cameron. Anger at the officers who had let Slim slip through their fingers, and relief at the realization that their carelessness had, in effect, freed him to pursue his personal agenda.

"Okay, Steve," he replied wearily, made tired by the inner conflict. "Keep me informed."

"Will do."

For long moments after the connection was severed, Cameron stood staring sightlessly at the instrument, examining possible approaches to take in bridging the widening chasm between him and Sandra.

How had it all started, anyway?

He shook his head, a frown knitting his brows, and glared at the innocent white instrument.

Oh, yeah, he had accused her, first of being childish, then of extreme militancy.

Dumb, Wolfe. Real dumb, because now he had to come up with a way to undo the damage.

As he turned from the phone, his glance collided with the kitchen table.

Telling himself that the first step in damage control had better start right there, he got busy cleaning up the breakfast dishes.

Some fifteen or so minutes later, Cameron found Sandra in the living room, staring out the window at the overcast but obviously milder day. He cleared his throat to draw her attention.

"More bad news?" she asked, not even bothering to turn and face him.

"No, just the opposite." Suddenly determined to have her look at him, he offered nothing more. His ploy worked; she turned to level a skeptical look at him.

The sight of her caused a strange and unfamiliar sensation inside him. For a moment, he simply stared at her, the look of her, feeling scared, deep in the pit of his stomach.

Except for Saturday evening, when they had both spruced up a bit for dinner, Sandra had dressed casually in old jeans and what looked like even older pullovers and shirts. She also had not bothered with makeup, except for a light application of protective moisturizer.

Now, the coolly composed woman facing him projected the image of a highly efficient professional lawyer—which, in fact, she was.

Though she was wearing jeans, they were neither old nor worn, but a slim-legged designer creation, with sharp, ironed-in creases. And, while she was wearing a shirt, it was silk, expensive, and tucked neatly into the belted jeans, the bottoms of which were tucked just as neatly into equally expensive black leather boots.

But that wasn't even the worst of it. Sandra's glowing, artifice-free appearance was gone, hidden behind a mask of expertly applied makeup.

She was breathtakingly beautiful, and appeared as removed from him, and the intimacy they had shared, as the sun appeared removed from the earth by the clouds.

"Let's not play silent games, Cameron." Her voice was as remote as her exquisite appearance. "If you have anything to say, say it."

Cameron tried a cajoling smile. "I thought, believed, we were both having a good time up until yesterday—playing games, I mean."

"That was then, and this is now." Not only did she not return his smile, her expression grew more severe. "And I'd appreciate it if you'd get on with it."

So much for cajolery, Cameron told himself derisively.

"Right," he said, shrugging in defeat. "From all indications, you are no longer in danger by remaining here in the cabin."

"The escaped criminal has been apprehended?"

"No." He shook his head. "It appears that Slim decided it was more to his advantage to make a run for it, instead of tracking me down to get even."

"But the manhunt is still on for him?"

"Of course."

"And you're free to go." Now she did smile, but it had hopeless finality in it, and he despaired when he saw it. "Go ahead." She waved a hand. "Go join the hunt."

"Sandra—" he began, but that was as far as she allowed him to go.

"Get going," she insisted. "It's not only your job, it's what you want to do. So, go do it."

"They don't need me." He raked a hand through his hair in frustration. "Dammit! You know the only reason I felt I should remain here alone was that there was reason to believe he was tracking me. I don't want to leave here. I don't want to leave you."

"I think, in effect, you already have." She shrugged. "I believe we parted company yesterday."

"Sandra..." he began again, feeling like an idiot, standing in the middle of the room. "Can't we at least sit down...talk about it?"

She hesitated, a tiny frown marring the perfection of her face, giving him an assessing once-over. "I don't see how talking will—"

He interrupted her with a hoarse plea. "Please."

She sighed, then shrugged, then nodded—much to his fervent relief.

Springing into action, Cameron whipped around to yank the bunched-up comforter from the sofa.

Sandra chose to sit down in the chair farthest from his makeshift bed.

Cameron ground his teeth, but accepted her choice without a murmur... or a whimper.

"All right, we're seated," she said, pointing out the obvious. "Talk."

Talk.

Right.

Damn.

Cameron felt as tongue-tied as a teenager on a first date, and about as graceless. Nevertheless, desperate, he launched into speech.

"I don't suppose you'd allow me a few minutes to shave, shower and get into clean clothes?" he said, keenly aware of his grungy appearance in comparison to her perfection. "Or at least brush my teeth?"

She moved to get up.

"Okay, forget it," he said, motioning to her to remain where she was. "I'll do it later."

She sat back and crossed her legs, reminding him of the day, a mere two weeks ago, but seemingly a lifetime, when she had come to his office to inform him that she was taking a leave of absence from her work.

Only then, Sandra had been friendly.

Now, while she was not openly hostile, she wasn't exactly friendly, either.

"Cameron, I'm developing a headache waiting for you to begin talking," she said impatiently.

Nudged into speaking, he blurted out artlessly, "I want to apologize. I'm sorry for accusing you of being childish and militant."

She smiled.

He winced at the derisive curve to her lips, lips that he longed to crush with his own—immediately after he scrubbed his teeth.

"Sandra, say something."

"What would you like me to say?" She raised her brows. "That I forgive you for saying what you so obviously believe?"

"I don't believe it." He gave a sharp shake of his head. "I was angry, and—"

She silenced him with a quick wave of her hand. "You were angry, and voicing the truth—according to Special Agent Cameron Wolfe."

"No! I—"

She again interrupted him. "But that doesn't matter. What matters is that it's clear we have no basis to continue this, er, relationship—" she grimaced "—for want of a better phrase."

"No basis?" Cameron laughed; he couldn't help it, despite the expanding feeling of dread inside him. "Sandra, we have spent over a week laughing, talking, loving and relating very well to each other."

"Yes," she readily agreed.

He began a hefty sigh of relief; she proceeded to steal his breath and quash his revived hope.

"But that was a time out of time," she continued, a faint, sad smile shadowing her lips. "It was an illusion, unrelated to reality, a game of 'Let's pretend.'" Then she sighed, and it held the sound not of relief, but of impending doom—his. "But life has a way of intruding, Cameron, shattering pretense and illusion with the ruthless blow of reality."

"Dammit, Sandra, that's ridiculous!" he exclaimed, springing up to go to her. "You and I—especially you and I, considering the work we do—deal in reality as a way of life." He performed his signature habit of spearing his long fingers into his sun-kissed hair. "Intrude? Hell, reality's there, a constant, in both our lives. And you know it."

"Yes, but—"

Now he would not allow her to finish. "But nothing. So we grabbed some time, time to relax, laugh, play, some time for ourselves, and for each other. Where's the illusion in that, the pretense?''

"It wasn't real, Cameron." She raised a hand to massage her temple. "It was fun and games. And you and I—especially you and I—know better than most that life is not fun and games. Reality is everyday, and the everyday Cameron and Sandra are two entirely different types, too different to coexist together every day."

"That's nuts!" He was forced to back up as she stood to face him squarely.

"No," she said sadly. "That's life."

The scared sensation in his stomach spread, permeating his being. "Sandra..." he began, afraid to ask, yet needing to know. "Are you saying that you don't want to continue exploring our relationship after we leave here?"

"What would be the point?" She shrugged, causing the silk to shimmer over her breasts, and the nerves to quiver throughout his body. "There is no genuine relationship to explore."

"No relationship?" He stared at her in disbelief and amazement, and was forced to fight an urgent impulse to grab her shoulders and shake her, or kiss her, or do something even more exciting—even if also reprehensible, under the circumstances. "You can't be serious."

"All right! There was a relationship...of sorts." Her composure, her even tone, revealed strain for the first time, encouraging Cameron for a moment. "But it was the stuff of kids playing house." She held up a hand when he would have objected. "There was no genuine communication, no mutual understanding."

"Uh-huh." Cameron heaved a tired sigh. "Square one. We're back to my rash and thoughtless charge of childishness and militant feminism."

"No!" she began, but then she echoed his weary sigh. "Yes, we're back to that—that, and the complete lack of understanding revealed by it."

"I told you I was angry."

"I know."

"And I was talking off the top of my head," he went on, asking himself whether he should confess to the fear for her safety that had fired his anger.

"And I firmly believe you were voicing your mind and your convictions."

"Sandra, no—"

"And that's fine," she continued, as if he hadn't spoken. "You're entitled to them. The problem is, they're invalid, at least from my perspective. Which is a solid indication that we merely spent a week out of time, indulging our senses in our sensual sabbatical, while not learning a damn thing about each other."

Now Cameron was developing a headache. Very likely, he concluded, from beating his head against the brick wall of Sandra's obstinacy.

"You're wrong," he insisted, refusing to give up, out of a sickening fear of losing her completely. "I have never felt more connected to a woman. And I mean mentally, as well as physically." He succumbed to the need to reach out, touch the tip of his fingers to her smooth cheek. "I thought, believed, you felt the same."

"I did," she whispered. "But..." She shook her head, dislodging his hand, his fingertips. "I...I don't know." She again massaged her temple. "I need time to think. Time alone." She stepped back. "I need breathing space, and distance. I need to go home."

"You can't," he reminded her. "At least not until we see what Whitfield is up to." He knew he had erred, and badly, even before he was finished.

She stiffened, and stepped away from him. "I'm a big girl now, and I can take care of myself. If I deem it necessary, I'll have a restraining order issued against Whitfield. But, for now, my headache's worse. I'm going to take a couple of aspirin and lie down."

"Sandra, wait," he pleaded when she turned and headed for the bedroom.

"If I fall asleep, I may well be in for the night," she said, as if he hadn't uttered a word.

"Sandra!"

"There is one more thing," she said, finally pausing in the archway to glance back at him.

"Yes?" he asked, with unabashed eagerness.

"I was listening to the radio this morning before you woke up. The weather service predicted that the temperature will continue to rise through this afternoon and tonight. By tomorrow morning, this ice will be gone." She hesitated briefly before adding, "And so will I."

Nine

———

Sandra was nearly finished packing her things by the time a beautiful spring dawn had bathed the landscape in tones of pearlized pink.

Unsurprisingly, after two nights of practically no sleep at all, she had fallen into a deep slumber mere minutes after swallowing two aspirin, then crawling into the too-empty bed. And she had slept straight through the rest of the afternoon and most of the night.

She had awoken rested and refreshed shortly before four a.m., her headache, if not her heartache, gone.

Finally, showered, dressed, and everything packed except for her makeup, Sandra stacked the stuff next to the bedroom door, then reluctantly left the room to face the by-then-bright sunlit day—and the sleeping Wolfe in the living room.

The living room was empty; the Wolfe was on the prowl in the kitchen. And the sight of him brought her up short in the doorway.

Barefoot, clad in faded jeans and a sweatshirt, both rumpled from being slept in—it was immediately obvious that he had slept, because he still looked groggy—his golden mane tousled, he looked totally disreputable and, to her admittedly biased eyes, absolutely delicious.

Although Sandra would have sworn her movements were noiseless, Cameron must have heard her—sensed her? smelled her?—for without so much as a glance over his shoulder, he muttered an invitation of sorts.

"Come have some coffee."

The weary sound of his voice undermined her determination and composure. There was a thread of near-defeat woven through his quiet tone that pierced her heart like a spear.

Defeat? Sandra asked herself, hovering uncertainly in the doorway. Cameron?

Get real.

Reacting to the mental gibe, she squared her shoulders and crossed the room to accept the steaming cup he turned to offer her.

"Thanks." Though her voice was steady, her fingers were not; she hid the tremor by wrapping them around the warm cup.

"You're welcome," he murmured, turning back to attend to the pans on the stove. "I was just about ready to scramble some eggs. Do you want some?"

"Yes, please." Despairing at the crack in her voice, she raised the cup to her lips to sip the hot brew, in the hope of relieving the parched feel in her throat.

"Potatoes, too?" He didn't glance around, but busied himself with prodding the potatoes with a spatula.

"Yes." It was all so banal, Sandra had to will herself to keep from shouting her answer at him, merely to see if he'd respond in kind.

"Okay. You can make the toast."

Make the toast? she thought, rather wildly. She felt as if she were toast.

Nevertheless, she set her cup on the countertop and moved to comply.

Breakfast was less than scintillating. It appeared that, after a week of chattering nonstop to one another, they had both run dry of conversation.

Well . . . perhaps not completely dry.

"You're really set on leaving today," Cameron said, shoving his plate aside. "Aren't you?"

"Yes, I am." Sandra sighed, now wishing the conversational stream had remained dry. "I'm packed and ready to go."

"Uh-huh." His sigh echoed hers. "And nothing I can say will change your mind?"

"No." She shook her head, and blamed the abrupt motion for the sting in her eyes. "I told you yesterday, I need some thinking time, alone..." She tried to smile; it didn't work; she gave it up. "Without distractions."

"Then you admit that I distract you?" Cameron's voice held a note of hope.

"Yes, of course, you know you do," she said, then hastened to quash the expectancy that flared in his blue eyes, "But, distraction aside, I still need time." She actually felt his expression of deflation, yet she proceeded in her determination. "And I'm taking it."

The fire dimmed in his beautiful eyes, leaving them lackluster. His expression set into a mask of control. "Do you have any idea how much time you'll need?" His voice was devoid of emotion or inflection.

"No."

"I see." He sighed, and a tiny nonsmile curved his lips. "Were you planning to let me know when—or if—you've reached a decision?"

"Yes, of course, I—"

"That's the second time you've said that," he said, interrupting impatiently. "And there's no damned 'of course' about it." He expelled a short laugh that had more the sound of a snort. "I really thought, believed, that I knew you, understood you, but—"

Sandra interrupted him. "That's exactly what I'm saying. We don't really know each other."

"But we could," he said in a flat voice. "If we wanted to make the effort." He pushed his chair back and stood up. "I do."

Struck by his implication that she was the one unwilling to make the effort, Sandra was swept by conflicting waves of anger and despair.

It was unfair, she cried in silent protest. He was being unfair, considering that it was he who had misread her.

"And, by your very silence, I must conclude that you don't want to make the effort."

"And, naturally, your conclusions are always correct," she retorted, smarting anew at his previous assumptions and accusations as to her motives.

"Not hardly," he retorted cynically. "At least, not where women are concerned."

Now anger was gaining the upper hand. How dare he cast her in the mold of the woman who had dumped him? Sandra railed. And dumped him for monetary reasons, at that!

"You know practically nothing about women," she said, scraping her own chair backward and rising to challenge him, stare for stare. She even managed a credible curl to her upper lip. "Other than their performance in bed."

"That was below the belt, Sandra," he told her. "Literally, as well as figuratively."

Shamed by her hasty and ill-considered barb, Sandra felt honor-bound to concede. "I know, and anger is no excuse for dirty pool. I'm sorry."

"Yeah, so am I." He moved his shoulders in a tired-looking shrug, and began gathering the dishes and flatware. "I guess we'd better clean up. If you're going, I might as well leave, too." He turned away, then glanced back at her. "Would you allow me to use the bedroom and bath to shower and get my stuff together?"

"Yes, certainly." She circled the table to relieve him of the dishes in his hands. "You can use them now. I'll clean up in here, and in the living room."

"Thanks." With a fleeting half smile, he relinquished the dishes, then strode from the room.

Sandra stood still, staring after him long after he had disappeared from view.

Had she made the right decision? she asked herself, gnawing on her lower lip. Was she doing what was best for both of them by sticking to that decision?

She loved him so very much. And she was now hurting so very badly. Perhaps...

Sandra brought her thoughts to a dead stop. Everything had happened too soon. Their relationship had become too intimate, too hot, too intense, much too quickly. She needed time, they both needed time, to ponder, to reevaluate their respective feelings before continuing on together.

A breathing spell was needed at this juncture, she advised herself. Perhaps, after a week or two of some serious soul-searching, and rational, detached thinking... Who knew?

Sandra sighed as she went about the business of putting Barbara's getaway house in order.

One thing was certain. She hoped, prayed, that eventually she and Cameron could reach a mutually satisfying solution. Because she wasn't sure she could stand spending the rest of her life without him being a part of it. Whereas once she had enjoyed being alone, now, since being with him, a part of him, sharing both love and laughter with him, to be forever without him was unthinkable.

Hell, she missed him already.

The living room had been put to rights and Sandra was finishing up in the kitchen when Cameron exited the bedroom, loaded down with his own and her luggage.

"If you'll get me your keys, I'll stash this stuff in the cars."

"Okay." Leaving the kitchen, she skirted around him and started for the bedroom to collect her handbag. "But don't try to lug all of it yourself," she called back to him. "I'll do my share."

With them working together in silence, the chore was swiftly accomplished. Everything was stashed in their respective vehicles, except for their jackets. Cameron tossed his onto one corner of the sofa. Sandra draped hers, along with her handbag, at the other end, fully aware of the symbolism of the distance separating the two garments.

"Is there any coffee left?" he asked, not looking at her as he walked around her, into the kitchen and directly to the coffeemaker on the countertop. "I'd like a cup before we leave."

"Yes, I saved it for you," she answered, devouring the look of him with her eyes as she trailed along after him, while trying to appear unaffected by the impact on her senses of the sight of him. "It's still hot."

"Good. Thanks." He glanced over his shoulder and offered her a real smile.

She gratefully accepted and returned his offering. "You're welcome."

She watched him hungrily while he poured out a cup of the dark liquid, quivering inside in response to the sheer masculine appeal of him. Attired in fresh jeans, a loose-knit white sweater and rugged boots, with his burnished hair gleaming from the shower and his face smooth from the razor, he was a sight to set any woman's heart aflutter.

Was she certifiably out of her mind in demanding that they part for a while, in denying herself the thrill and pleasure of his exciting company?

Possibly, but . . .

Sandra's thoughts fractured as, at that moment, Cameron leaned forward, then went completely still, peering intently out the window above the sink overlooking the deck and the foothills beyond.

"Cameron, what—"

"Son of a—" His muttered curse cut across her voice as he suddenly set the cup on the countertop and strode to the back door.

Blinking in surprise and puzzlement, she watched him twist the lock, swing the door open and then stride out onto the deck.

Intrigued by his curious and abrupt action, she set her own cup on the table and followed him.

He was hunkered down in the center of the deck, staring intently at the floor.

"Cameron, what is it?" she asked, coming up beside him. "What's wrong?"

"That," he answered tersely, pointing at a muddy footprint on the floor. "And those," he added, indicating several other prints leading to and away from the window. "Seems we had a visitor during the night, or very early this morning."

A chill ran up Sandra's spine, and she shivered in reaction. "A visitor? Who?" she asked in a near-whisper, even though she feared she knew.

Cameron sliced a droll look at her. "That's the print of a cowboy boot." He got up to examine the other footprints. "And I'd say it was a safe bet it and the others were made by our friend Slim."

"But..." Sandra had to pause to wet her suddenly parched lips. "I thought the authorities were certain he had fled to the area around Taos, New Mexico," she said, glancing uneasily around her.

"A wily son of a bitch, is our Slim." His lips twisted in disgust. "Apparently he gave them the slip again." Pivoting, he crossed the deck to her, grasped her arm and hustled her to the door. "Let's get back inside," he ordered, literally shoving her through the doorway. "We're exposed here."

Her thoughts exactly, Sandra thought, clasping her arms around her body to contain a shudder.

Cameron headed straight for the wall phone, punched in a number, then stood, stiff and alert, staring out the window through narrowed, glittering eyes.

"It's Wolfe," she heard him say into the receiver. "And I think my tracker has found me."

Not waiting to hear any more, she walked into the living room and pulled on her jacket. She was doing up the buttons when he came into the room.

"What are you doing?"

"Getting ready," she answered, frowning at the authoritarian note in his voice. "We are leaving at once, aren't we?"

"No, Sandra," he said, moving around her to get to his own jacket. "You're not going anywhere. Not as long as he's skulking about out there."

"But then, why are you putting on your jacket?" she asked, then exclaimed, "Oh!" when he thrust a hand beneath the end sofa cushion and withdrew a holstered pistol. She took a step back. "I hate guns."

"So do I." A tired smile feathered his lips at the look of revulsion on her face. "I especially hate them when they're in the hands of criminals."

"You're going out there, looking for him." Sandra moistened her lips. "Aren't you?"

"Of course," he snapped, drawing the weapon from the holster. He tossed the harness onto the sofa, then raised his intent blue eyes to her. "It's my job."

"But... but..." she sputtered, watching him shrug into his jacket. "You can't go out there after him alone!" She reached out impulsively to grab his arm.

"Can't I?" He shook off her hand and moved away from her. "Watch me."

"Cameron, please," she pleaded, frantic with fear for him. "At least wait for backup."

Shaking his head, he walked into the kitchen and to the back door. "I won't take a chance on being pinned down in here. If there's going to be any more hunting done, then I'm going to do it."

She was right on his heels, her heart racing, her eyes wide and frightened. Dipping his head, he brushed a kiss across her parted lips, then opened the door.

"Lock this at once," he ordered, leveling a scorching, memorizing look on her face. "Stay inside, and away from the windows, until I return."

Obeying instinctively, Sandra locked the door the instant he closed it. Then she ran to the kitchen window, a shiver skittering up her spine as she watched Cameron swiftly cross the deck, descend the steps and follow the trail of boot prints into the wooded foothills.

The Lone Wolfe was on the hunt.

Crouched low, and moving fast, Cameron followed the boot tracks across the open area next to the house, then into the trees at the base of the foothills.

Even with the undergrowth, he had little difficulty discerning the erratic trail Slim had left.

Moving slower, but at a steady pace, he followed the zigzag, circling path delineated by the indentations in the rain-softened earth from the distinctive slanted-heeled, pointy-toed cowboy boot.

It was tough going, and time-consuming, but after what Cameron judged to have been in actual measure approximately three-quarters of a mile, the tracks intersected a narrow, rutted roadway. There the boot tracks proceeded on a straight course, deeper into the woods, and to a small clearing, where a tree-scraped and battered van—likely stolen—was parked.

In the sylvan setting, all was quiet and serene; birds chittered and scolded each other in the treetops.

Cameron approached the vehicle with tense caution and bated breath. Stepping gingerly, so as not to dislodge a stone or crunch a twig, he moved up to the rear of the van, then along its closed side panels.

Pausing behind the passenger-side door, he drew a silent breath, leaned forward for a quick peek inside, then, finding the front seats empty, pulled back.

Preparing to move on the count of three, he tightened his grip on the gun, drew another, deeper breath, then counted—one, two, three, go!

His movements fast, sure, Cameron stepped forward, grasped the door handle with his left hand, pulled it open and burst into the front of the van, right arm extended to the rear, finger taut on the trigger.

The van was empty.

The pent-up breath whooshed out of him in a harsh exhalation. But, although the interior was devoid of life, there were clear signs of Slim's occupancy.

An open heavy-duty sleeping bag lay along one wall. Two six-packs of bottled beer, one empty, were set close to it, along with a crumpled potato chip bag, a package of cookies and a half-full milk container. Two plastic sandwich bags, both with the remnants of sandwiches inside, littered the floor.

Cameron drew a breath, and wrinkled his nose at the strong smell of beer. The strength of the odor gave evidence of Slim's recent presence.

Unease unfurled in his stomach. Slim had been here, at least long enough to eat and swig some beer. And then he had left again, to go—

Sandra!

Stark fear clutching at his throat, Cameron scrambled back from the van, then circled around the front, to the driver's side. The mark of a boot heel was deep in the ground where Slim had stepped out. From there, the tracks led off, across the makeshift road and into the woods, back in the direction of the cabin.

"Goddamn."

Muttering the curse, along with several other inventive and profane utterances, Cameron took off at a watchful trot, following the trail of boot prints.

It led straight back to the cabin.

Standing at the edge of the tree line, yet concealed by the trees, his eyes crawling inch by inch, Cameron surveyed the terrain, and the situation. His gaze paused for long moments on the two vehicles, Sandra's compact and his own larger four-wheel, parked, his behind hers, in front of the cabin. There was not a shadow, not a hint of motion. All appeared peaceful, serene, in the warm midmorning spring sunlight.

There was not a sign of Slim—outside.

The short hairs at the back of Cameron's neck quivered as his gaze came to a halt on the cabin.

Although the clearing between the house and the trees was relatively short in distance, it was a decidedly far piece in time of exposure. He knew he'd be a sitting duck if he should leave the protective cover.

And yet, if Slim had somehow managed to gain entrance into the cabin, to Sandra...

Cameron stopped thinking and started moving.

He had traversed about three-quarters of the distance to the house, and was drawing even with the cars, when he caught a flicker of movement from the far side of his vehicle out of the corner of his eye.

He spun instinctively to face the possible danger. His sudden movement saved his life.

In what seemed like fast-forward action, Cameron saw Slim rise to his full height and fire off a shot from his hastily raised rifle.

The bullet missed Cameron's head by a fraction of an inch.

The sickening crack of the rifle shot halted Sandra in her tracks in the center of the living room, where she had been pacing since moments after Cameron had left the house. She had filled those moments by running into the bedroom to retrieve the pistol she had shoved to the back of the bedside table drawer, behind her paperback books.

The awful sound of gunfire had come from the front of the house.

Cameron!

Clutching the detested weapon in a trembling hand, Sandra dashed to the door, disengaged the lock and, unmindful of her own safety, yanked open the door and ran onto the porch.

The tableau that confronted her wide eyes sent her heartbeat into overdrive and her blood surging like ice water through her veins.

Cameron stood in the clearing near the cabin, exposed to the man standing on the far side of the large vehicle, caught in the cross hairs of the rifle nestled against his shoulder.

Sandra didn't pause to think or consider. Raising her arms and thrusting them out straight, she wrapped her left hand around her right on the butt of the handgun, took aim, held her breath and eased back the trigger.

She missed her target by a hair.

Still, her instinctive action saved the day, and her lover's life.

Zinging by as close as it did, the shot naturally distracted Slim for an instant. An instant was all Cameron required. Raising his own weapon, he took careful aim and fired.

He didn't miss. The bullet rocketed straight through Slim's right shoulder. The rifle fell to the ground. Slim followed it down. He didn't make it to the ground; he crumpled over the hood of the vehicle.

Across the short distance separating them, Sandra and Cameron stared at each other. He took two steps toward her, then stopped, slicing a look at Slim. The criminal groaned; Cameron steadied his aim on him.

At that moment, three cars, two with official emblems emblazoned on their white sides, tore, sirens wailing, up the private road. The sight of them broke the shock gripping Sandra.

She had almost killed a man!

The stark realization of how very close she had come, how very much she had wanted to take the life of another human being, made her feel physically ill.

Home. She had to go home.

The directive ringing in her head, a sob clawing at her throat, she lowered her still stiffly outstretched arms, turned and ran into the house.

Refusing to pause to think, to consider her actions or her reactions, she grabbed her jacket and dug in her handbag for car and house keys. Then, dropping the key to the cabin on the shoulder holster, she whirled and ran from the house, down the porch steps, and to her car.

"Sandra!"

Drawing in shuddering breaths, she ignored Cameron's call. Firing the engine, she turned the compact in a tight U-turn and drove down the road.

Sandra didn't so much as glance at the men standing along the side of the road, staring at her. She didn't even glance in the rearview mirror for a backward look.

She had told Cameron she needed thinking time. Now, after being willing—no, determined—to destroy a life to preserve the life of the man she loved, she needed that time more than before.

She'd deal with it, Sandra knew. But she'd deal
with it in her own time, in her own way.

At home.

Cameron knew where to find her.

Ten

___

Why hadn't they stayed in bed together?

The thought drifted into Cameron's mind as he stood in the open doorway to Sandra's apartment. A pang of regret clutched at his chest as his eyes noted the paleness of her cheeks, the dark smudges beneath her soft eyes.

Damn. What had he done to her?

"Hi, Annie Oakley," he said, his voice sounding strained to his own ears. "May I come in?"

A faint wisp of a smile touched her lips, and his heart, at his teasing gibe. Hope soared inside him when she nodded and stepped back, allowing him entrance.

"I missed you like hell this past week and a half," he confessed, gently closing the door behind him.

"But you didn't call, or stop by," Sandra said, motioning him into the living room.

"I was giving you the time you asked for," he said, absently taking in the clean, elegant, yet comfortable-looking decor of her home. "But I couldn't wait any longer," he admitted, offering her a coaxing smile. "I needed to see you."

"Oh, that's right, you're leaving for Pennsylvania soon." Her answering smile held acceptance. "For your brother's wedding. Jake, right?"

"Yes, but that isn't why I needed to see you." Cameron took a careful step, closing the distance between them. "I had to make certain you were all right." The evidence of her wan appearance convinced him she wasn't. "Are you having guilt fits about firing on Slim?"

"No." Sandra's voice held relieving conviction. "I read in the paper that he survived your shot."

"I planned it that way." Cameron frowned, deciding to clear up any misconceptions she might be harboring. "I don't get my kicks from killing, Sandra."

Her eyes flew wide. "I never believed you did!" she exclaimed. "Why did you think I had?"

"You hate guns."

"Yes, but..." Her voice faded, and she shrugged. "I knew what you did for a living."

He heaved a sigh. "I'm glad that's cleared up—it did have me concerned." He hazarded another step closer. "Now I'd like to clear up something else."

She didn't back away. She did arch her brows questioningly.

"It doesn't take a brick building to fall on me," he said, his tone rife with self-derision. "All it took was the sound of a gunshot."

She frowned. "I don't understand."

"Neither did I." He held his breath and took another step, bringing him to within two feet of her. "I mean, I didn't understand until then the reason you were so angry and impatient with me."

"And now you do?" She remained still.

"Hmm..." He nodded, and took a chance on touching her—just the tip of his fingers to the curve of her pale cheek; it felt like satin. Desire twisted inside him. He tamped it down, cautioning himself against screwing up.

Sandra shivered.

Encouraged, Cameron explained, "I now believe that you weren't angry because I accused you of being childish and bent out of shape about having your autonomy questioned. You were angry because I was so damn dense. I misunderstood your concern for me, my safety." He paused, then asked, "Right?" Then he held his breath.

"Yes." She smiled. "Now, will you tell me how the sound of a gunshot brought the revelation?"

The pent-up breath eased from his taut body. "Simple. You hate guns, and yet you not only handled one, but fired it with intent in defense of me."

"And I'd do it again."

Just five words, spoken with quiet conviction. Five beautiful words. Elation swept through Cameron, banishing his fear of her rejection. He took the final step necessary to sweep her into his embrace.

Sandra, his Sandra, the cool, professional, ofttimes militant lady lawyer, felt so fragile, so very delicate, lying passive against him. Cameron felt a powerful need to shelter her with his arms, protect her with his life, and adore her forever with his body.

He tightened his arms around her now trembling body, and buried his face in her scented sable hair.

Her arms curled tightly around his waist and, murmuring his name, she pressed her lips to the side of his neck.

"I love you." Cameron scoured his mind for stronger words, but there was no other way to say it. No way to dress it up, give it flourish. "Sandra, I love you."

"I love you back." She tilted her head to gaze into his eyes. "Cameron, I love you so much."

Although it was a short distance from the living room to Sandra's bedroom, it was much too far for two people, deeply in love, who had not seen each other, touched each other, kissed each other, for over a week.

As if by mutual, spoken consent, clothes were quickly discarded and they sank as one to the thickly piled springy carpet.

Mouths touched, teased, fused. Tongues tasted, dueled, plunged. Hands caressed, tormented, urged. Finally, finally, bodies angled, positioned, merged.

The coming together was glorious.

A spring storm raged overhead as Cameron cradled Sandra in his arms and carried her to bed.

Neither of them heard the storm—they were too involved in creating one of their own.

Their passion abated as the storm moved east. Exhausted, entwined in each other's arms, Cameron and Sandra fell headfirst into the sleep of utter satisfaction and contentment.

An increasingly persistent call of nature woke Sandra several hours later. Sighing in resignation, she slipped noiselessly from the bed and went into the bathroom.

Although her period was late by only a few days, the nearly constant sensation of needing to seek relief, along with the extreme tenderness in her breasts, had convinced Sandra that she had conceived Cameron's baby.

At first, she had dismissed the idea as secret wishful thinking, reminding herself how careful Cameron had been to ensure protection.

Then she had had vivid recall of their encounters of the sensual kind while in the shower, when all thoughts and consideration of protection had been washed away by the flush of passion.

Now, experiencing her first twinge of nausea, Sandra knew without doubt that she was pregnant. Pleasure suffused her being, brought color to her cheeks and a sparkle of anticipation to her eyes.

Her baby.

Cameron's baby.

Their baby.

Nature's business taken care of, Sandra brushed her teeth, then hummed a lullaby while she luxuriated under a warm shower spray. Refreshed, excited by her secret, she sauntered into the bedroom, crawled back into bed and snuggled close to the warm body of her lover.

"Where were you?" Cameron growled in a loving tone, coiling one strong arm around her waist to draw her tightly to him. "I missed you."

"Good." Asking herself if she should tell him, share her secret with him, she planted a kiss on his smooth, golden-hair-sprinkled chest.

He didn't give her time to tell him anything. Moving with the swiftness of the animal whose name he bore, he heaved himself up and over her.

"Good? I'll show you good," he purred.

And he did. She enjoyed every heated, open-mouthed kiss, every stroke of hand and tongue, every deep thrust of his taut body.

When it was over, and their shudders of ecstasy had slowly subsided, Sandra was spent, but exhilarated by the heady sensation of sheer feminine power.

Yes, she decided, she'd tell him. Forming the words in her head, she began, "Cam—"

"Wolves mate for life, you know," he said, raising his head to stare at her.

"Yes, I know," she said, the gleam in his blue eyes setting her pulses thundering.

"We've mated."

"Yes." A strange excitement robbed her voice of substance, making it sound whispery, barely there. "I...I know."

"Then, my sweet mate, I think you'll have to come with me to Pennsylvania." His voice held little more substance than hers. "Because I can't face the thought of being away from my mate for another week or so." The intent look in his eyes softened to one of entreaty. "Will you come with me, meet the rest of the Wolfe pack?"

"You just try to go anywhere without me," she said in a credible growl. Lifting her head, she caught his mouth in a long, hard, possessive kiss. "From now on, your Lone Wolfe days are over, Cameron Wolfe."

His laughter ringing joyously inside her head, Cameron returned her kiss with interest.

All together in one room, the Wolfe pack were more than a little overpowering.

Naturally, Sandra immediately took a liking to each and every one of them; how could she not? Though distinct and individual, each and every one of them was very much like Cameron. Tall, muscular, blond and blue-eyed, the four brothers presented a formidable, devastatingly handsome picture to the world in general—and four vastly different females in particular.

But there was one woman in the room who appeared neither impressed nor intimidated, Sandra noted with an inner smile.

Maddy Wolfe was decidedly the unopposed leader of this particular pack.

Sandra had liked Maddy from the moment Cameron proudly introduced his mother to her. Maddy was warm and welcoming, and had opened her home, and her arms, to Sandra, bestowing a brilliant smile and a quick hug on the younger woman. That had been two days ago.

At the time, Maddy had been alone in the house, which had afforded Sandra some time to get to know the other woman. It hadn't taken very long for Sandra to realize from whom Cameron had learned to be a many-faceted person, as well as a man.

That evening, Sandra had met Cameron's youngest brother, Jake, and his prospective bride, Sarah, a lovely young woman of keen intelligence and humor.

The following day, Eric had arrived, escorting his lady, Tina, who also was lovely, and intelligent, with a different, but obvious, sense of humor.

The day after that, Royce had appeared, with yet another lovely and intelligent woman in tow. Her name was Megan. She was flat-out gorgeous and intelligent, with a lively sense of humor.

Since it had turned out that, whenever they were confined together, the four brothers happily traded gibes, quips and dryly delivered insults, Sandra had decided that it was a good thing that their respective female companions all possessed a healthy sense of humor—seeing as how she couldn't imagine how they could survive otherwise.

Laughter, feminine and masculine, rang through the house. Through it all, Maddy's eyes danced with pleasure at the antics of her tall sons, and at the gentle ripostes of the younger women.

Being the only child of parents cool to emotional displays, Sandra soaked up the roisterous exchange of love and laughter like a dry sponge. She couldn't help but notice that Sarah, Tina and Megan were likewise basking in the warmth freely given by the Wolfes.

Sandra was glad she had agreed to come east with Cameron, for several reasons, the uppermost of them the whole new look and perception she received of him as he related with his family.

The Cameron she had come to know was shrewd and tough and passionate, with moments of tenderness and gentleness. The man she observed in his mother's home was the same, but with a larger, fuller personality. He was caretaker and caregiver, the son who had stepped forth to fill the gap when his strong father, Justin Wolfe, died in the line of duty.

Sandra already loved Cameron. Yet, though she would not have believed it possible, after she saw him in the role of loving son and supportive brother, the love she felt for him deepened, expanded, became all-encompassing.

Here was a man to hitch a life to.

Within two uproarious days, the assembled men and women were all chattering together like a bunch of magpies, as if they had all known each other for years.

Sandra was enjoying herself so much, she barely noticed the continuing off-and-on moments of queasiness in her stomach.

But when the nausea struck at quiet times, when she and Cameron were alone in the room they had taken in a motel just outside of town, it was a stinging reminder that she had not as yet shared her secret with him.

Although she no longer felt so much as a qualm concerning his reaction to her suspicion of pregnancy, she held off, waiting for the perfect moment to tell him he was going to be a father.

The Sunday before the wedding, they all gathered at Maddy's house for dinner. The men insisted on doing the cooking. The younger women insisted on helping. Maddy serenely directed the riotous proceedings.

It was great fun; Sandra enjoyed every minute of it, and happily raised her glass in a toast when Eric announced that he and Tina had decided to take the big step. Jake followed the announcement with one of his own, that he and Sarah were thrilled with Eric's suggestion to make it a double wedding.

After dinner, the men retired to the patio, ostensibly to discuss the new arrangements, but in reality to share a beer and rag each other.

It was late when Sandra and Cameron got back to their motel room. She was tired, but pleasantly so. He was amorous, but tenderly so.

Their loving was slow and gentle, sweet and endearing. When it was over, Cameron continued to stroke Sandra, loving her in a different way.

It was the perfect moment to share secrets. But, even as Sandra was again forming the words in her mind to tell him, Cameron confided two secrets of his own.

"It's going to be a triple wedding, you know," he said in an amusement-laced tone.

"Triple?" Sandra angled her head to stare up at him. "You mean Royce and Megan?"

"Yeah." He laughed. "He asked Jake and Eric if they'd mind while we were guzzling Mom's beer and lying to each other out on the patio after dinner."

Bemused, she laughed with him. "Does your mother know?"

He canted his head to give her a wry look. "Of course. Mom knows everything." He chuckled. "She also knows that all three of my future sisters-in-law are pregnant."

A thrill of sensation shot through Sandra. "All three of them?" she repeated, thinking the time had most definitely come for confession.

"Yes, and Mom's near delirious with excitement about it." He hesitated, stroking her hip. "Er . . . Sandra?"

"I have something to discuss with you," she said in a rush. "I hope—" that was as far as she got.

"I have something I want to ask you," he interrupted her to say in an attention-getting tone of urgency. He drew a breath, and then, staring intently into her eyes, quickly said, "Sandra, you know I love you very much, don't you?"

"Yes, but . . ."

"Do you love me? Really love me?"

"Cameron, you know I do!" she cried, made nervous by the intensity of his voice.

"Enough to marry me?" he asked in a rush, then appeared to hold his breath.

Sandra went still for an instant. Then sheer joy burst through her, out of her.

"Yes! Oh, Cameron, yes, yes, yes!"

He exhaled, grinned, then laughed aloud. "Oh, sweetheart, you can't imagine how scared I was to ask you, how scared I was you'd say no."

Frowning, she levered herself up, unconcerned about her nakedness, to scowl at him. "You, scared? It boggles the mind. Why would you even think I'd say no?"

"Well, honey, you're a professional, and all that." His smile was teasing. "A feminist."

She gave him a playful, but meaningful, punch on his bare shoulder.

He grabbed her and drew her mouth to his for a playful, but meaningful, kiss.

"We could make it a complete family affair," he slyly suggested. "I'm sure my brothers would be delighted with the idea."

She hesitated a moment longer, then drew a breath and took the plunge. "I suppose we might as well," she agreed. "Make it unanimous... in every aspect."

It took a frowning moment. Then Cameron's eyes flashed and widened.

"You're pregnant?"

"Well, I'm not absolutely certain yet... but I'm pretty certain."

"Sandra." He laughed. "Mom'll freak!"

"Yes, but what about you?" she asked, in a voice betraying uncertainty.

"Are you kidding?" He drew her to him, kissed her cheeks, her eyes, her nose, her mouth. "I'm already freaking. Oh, Sandra..." His voice got lost inside her mouth; it found a home in her heart.

Sandra placed a long-distance call early the next morning, to tell her parents the happy news.

There was not an unoccupied foot of space in the Sprucewood College campus chapel.

Resplendent in their bright spring finery, the female guests looked like blossoms strewn amid the more subdued shades of the gentlemen's suits and jackets.

Sunshine struck jewel tones of light through the stained-glass windows. A warm breeze wafted through the tilted panes.

Seated in the first pew, her eyes sparkling, her smile serene, Maddy turned her head to smile at the distinguished-looking couple seated opposite her across the aisle.

Sandra's parents, William and Lisa Bradley, had flown in from Paris just that morning. They were the only parents of the brides able to make the wedding.

Disappointed for the others, but happy for Sandra, Maddy nodded to the couple, then turned her gaze proudly upon her tall, stalwart, handsome blond sons.

Attired in navy blue suits, pristine white shirts and muted patterned neckties, the four brothers stood side by side in front of the small altar, facing but not seeing the assembled guests. All four pairs of gleaming blue eyes were fixed on the back of the chapel.

Jake looked nervous—but trying not to show it.

Eric looked too relaxed—a sure sign of nervousness.

Royce looked contained—another sure sign.

Cameron looked remote—a dead giveaway.

The Wolfe men were getting married—and were anxious about it.

A rustling murmur rippled through the chapel. An instant before she turned around, Maddy's eyes misted as she witnessed the blaze of love shining from the eyes of each one of her sons. A tear escaped her guard as she turned to look at the young women slowly pacing the distance along the aisle to the men.

Sarah was in the lead, her soft eyes riveted to Jake's.

Tina came second, her smile fixed on Eric.

Megan followed third, her face aglow for Royce.

Sandra was last, a picture of pure love for Cameron.

It was a beautiful quadruple wedding.

Every female cried; there were even tears in the eyes of some of the males.

The reception was more joyous and boisterous than the previous gatherings at Maddy's home. It was an absolute crush; there was only the tiniest space for dancing. No one seemed to mind.

Sandra loved every minute of it. But she wasn't sorry when, after a brief conference with his brothers, Cameron drew her aside to whisper, "Watches have been synchronized. In precisely thirty seconds, Jake, Eric, Royce and I are going to grab our wives and break out of this joint."

Sandra was breathless, and still laughing, long after she had kissed, and Cameron had shaken hands with, her parents, and all the others had all hugged Maddy in turn, then, calling their good-byes, literally run to their separate cars.

After the four of them had given a final wave to one another, the four vehicles took off in different directions.

Cameron swept her into his arms the moment he shut the motel-room door. "You're so beautiful," he murmured. Then, in the exact same way he had the day he arrived at the cabin, he swung her around, singing, "Dance with me, I want my arms about you..." He broke off to declare, "I love you, my beautiful wife."

"And I love you, my handsome husband," Sandra vowed, smiling up at him through the tears of happiness welling in her shining eyes.

Cameron brushed his lips over hers. "Oh, my love, I'm so glad this Wolfe won't be alone anymore."

*   *   *   *   *

Mrs. Maddy Wolfe

is

Proud. Delighted. Thrilled

to Announce

the Births of Her Grandchildren

Sons Born

Justin J. on February 3rd to Jake and Sarah

Mark E. on February 9th to Eric and Tina

Edward R. on February 17th to Royce and Megan

and

Two, Count 'Em, Two

Daughters!

Matilda and Lisa on February 20th to Cameron and Sandra

Hip, Hip, Hooray!

SILHOUETTE® Desire®

COMING NEXT MONTH

#979 MEGAN'S MARRIAGE—Annette Broadrick
Daughters of Texas
February's *Man of the Month* and Aqua Verde County's most
eligible bachelor, Travis Hanes, wanted Megan O'Brien as his
bride. And now that she needed his help, could Travis finally talk
stubborn Megan into being the wife he wanted?

#980 ASSIGNMENT: MARRIAGE—Jackie Merritt
Tuck Hannigan had to pose as pretty Nicole Currie's husband if
he was to protect her. Could this phony marriage get the
confirmed bachelor thinking about a honyemoon for real?

#981 REESE: THE UNTAMED—Susan Connell
Sons and Lovers
Notorious playboy Reese Marchand knew mysteriously sexy
Beth Langdon was trouble. But he couldn't stay away from the
long-legged beauty—even if it meant revealing his long-kept
secret.

#982 THIS IS MY CHILD—Lucy Gordon
Single dad Giles Haverill was the only man who could help
Melanie Haynes find the baby she'd been forced to give up
years ago. Unfortunately, he was also the one man she could
never love....

#983 DADDY'S CHOICE—Doreen Owens Malek
Taylor Kirkland's goal in life was to regain custody of his
daughter. But then he met Carol Lansing—an irresistible woman
whose love could cost him that dream....

#984 HUSBAND MATERIAL—Rita Rainville
Matthew Flint never thought he would make a good husband—
until he lost the only woman he ever loved. Now he would do
anything to convince Libby Cassidy he really was husband
material.

Bestselling author

RACHEL LEE

takes her Conard County series to new heights with

A CONARD COUNTY Reckoning

This March, Rachel Lee brings readers a brand-new, longer-length, out-of-series title featuring the characters from her successful Conard County miniseries.

Janet Tate and Abel Pierce have both been betrayed and carry deep, bitter memories. Brought together by great passion, they must learn to trust again.

"Conard County is a wonderful place to visit! Rachel Lee has crafted warm, enchanting stories. These are wonderful books to curl up with and read. I highly recommend them."
—*New York Times* bestselling author
Heather Graham Pozzessere

Available in March, wherever Silhouette books are sold.

It's our 1000th Special Edition and we're celebrating!

Join us these coming months for some wonderful stories in a special celebration of our 1000th book with some of your favorite authors!

Diana Palmer   **Nora Roberts**
Debbie Macomber **Christine Flynn**
Phyllis Halldorson **Lisa Jackson**

Plus miniseries by:

Lindsay McKenna, Marie Ferrarella, Sherryl Woods and Gina Ferris Wilkins.

And many more books by special writers!

And as a special bonus, all Silhouette Special Edition titles published during Celebration 1000! will have **_double_** Pages & Privileges proofs of purchase!

Silhouette Special Edition...heartwarming stories packed with emotion, just for you! You'll fall in love with our next 1000 special stories!

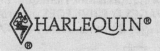

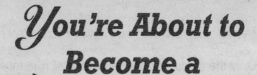

You're About to Become a

Privileged Woman

Reap the rewards of fabulous free gifts and benefits with proofs-of-purchase from Silhouette and Harlequin books

Pages & Privileges™

It's our way of thanking you for buying our books at your favorite retail stores.

PROOF OF PURCHASE
SD-PP91
Offer expires October 31, 1996

Pages & Privileges ™

Harlequin and Silhouette—
the most privileged readers in the world!

For more information about Harlequin and Silhouette's PAGES & PRIVILEGES program call the Pages & Privileges Benefits Desk: 1-503-794-2499

Silhouette®

SD-PP91